MARIE-MADELEINE PIOCHE DE LA VERGNE, COMTESSE DE LAFAYETTE, was born in Paris in 1634. Her father, governor of Le Havre, died when she was in her teens, and her mother then married the Baron Renaud de Sévigné. Thus she met Madame de Sévigné, who introduced her to court circles and with whom she remained intimate until her death. In 1655 Marie married Jean François Motier, the Comte de Lafayette, and retired for a time to his quiet estates in Auvergne, meanwhile corresponding eagerly with her former tutor, Gilles de Ménage, from whom she gleaned gossip of her beloved Paris and of court life. Under an amicable agreement with her husband, in 1659 Marie returned to Paris, where she became the intimate friend and companion of Duc de La Rochefoucauld, author of *Les Maximes*. Their affection continued until his death. Her first novel, *The Princess of Montpensier,* appeared anonymously in 1660, but neither it nor those that followed gave a hint of the quality of her masterpiece, *The Princess of Clèves* (1678). She remained in Paris, conducted her own salons, and became the friend of various people of the court, among whom were Jeanne de Nemours, the Duchess of Savoy, and Henrietta of England, the Duchess of Orléans. Her biography of the latter appeared several years after Madame de Lafayette's death in 1693.

WALTER J. COBB has translated several Signet Classics, including Flaubert's *Three Tales*.

NANCY K. MILLER is Distinguished Professor of English at Lehman College and the Graduate Center, CUNY.

THE
PRINCESS
OF CLÈVES

Madame de Lafayette

Newly Revised Translation by
Walter J. Cobb
Introduction by Nancy K. Miller

Updated Bibliography

A MERIDIAN CLASSIC

Published by the Penguin Group
Penguin Books USA Inc., 375 Hudson Street,
New York, New York 10014, U.S.A.
Penguin Books Ltd, 27 Wrights Lane,
London W8 5TZ, England
Penguin Books Australia Ltd, Ringwood,
Victoria, Australia
Penguin Books Canada Ltd, 10 Alcorn Ave.,
Toronto, Ontario, Canada M4V 3B2
Penguin Books (N.Z.) Ltd, 182-190 Wairau Road,
Auckland 10, New Zealand

Penguin Books Ltd, Registered Offices:
Harmondsworth, Middlesex, England

Published by Meridian Classic, an imprint of New American Library,
a division of Penguin Books USA Inc.

BOOKS ARE AVAILABLE AT QUANTITY DISCOUNTS WHEN
USED TO PROMOTE PRODUCTS OR SERVICES. FOR
INFORMATION PLEASE WRITE TO PREMIUM MARKETING
DIVISION, PENGUIN BOOKS USA INC., 375 HUDSON STREET,
NEW YORK, NEW YORK 10014

Library of Congress Catalog Card Number: 89-60749

 REGISTERED TRADEMARK—MARCA REGISTRADA

First Meridian Classic Printing, September, 1989

4   5   6   7   8   9   10   11   12

PRINTED IN CANADA

Contents

Introduction

In standard histories of French literature, *The Princess of Clèves* figures as a masterpiece of classical prose and as the origin of the modern psychological novel. In France, this brilliant historical fiction of love and politics in the sixteenth-century court of Henri II has long been part of the canon—the pantheon of "great works" that represents a national culture's ideas about its values and identity. In more recent history, *The Princess of Clèves* has become an essential text for critical discussions of women and literature; it is central to current efforts to determine the history and its consequences for the cultural record, of being a writer aware of being read as a woman. *The Princess of Clèves* thus makes two powerful and asymmetrical claims on contemporary attention: it is a major text in the dominant tradition of the European novel. It is a major novel in the body of works by women writers.

Should a woman tell her husband she is in love with another man? This was the question that seventeenth-century readers debated when *The Princess of Clèves* appeared anonymously in 1678. Lafayette's fiction of "ambition and gallantry," launched by an elaborate press campaign, immediately became not only a best-seller, but the subject of intense social contention and elaborate critical scrutiny. Readers of the *Mercure Galant*—a contemporary monthly—were invited to comment on the dilemma posed by the novel's plot, and for almost a year literary France pondered the proper course of action for a "virtuous woman tormented by a very great passion that she has tried to overcome by every possible means." More than three hundred years later, controversy about the novel's heroine and the conundrum of her life has yet to be definitively settled.

"Mme. de Clèves' confession to her husband," wrote the seventeenth-century critic Bussy-Rabutin to his cousin Madame de Sévigné in a semiprivate exchange of letters about the novel, "is extravagant, and can only be told in a true story; but when one is inventing a story for its own sake, it is ridiculous to ascribe such extraordinary feelings to one's heroine. In so doing, the author cared more about not resembling other novels than obeying common sense." The confession, Bussy complains, "is not plausible and smells of the novel." Bussy was both right and wrong (and right for the wrong reasons). In creating a heroine with such extraordinary feelings and designing an extravagant plot for her, Lafayette probably was more concerned with writing something original than respecting the maxims of common sense, but that—at least in part—is because common sense offered women no way out of the plots society had written for them. When the Princess of Clèves herself remarks upon the "singularity of such a confession—the like of which she had never heard" (101), she is also saying that her "extraordinary feelings" require a story that has never been told before. Lafayette's princess is a heroine dedicated to her singularity, and the important moments of the novel are marked by a challenge to the social and literary standards of plausibility in seventeenth-century France.

The princess's avowal to her husband is a link in the chain of events that lead inexorably to her decision not to marry, when she is free to do so, the only man she has ever loved. Bussy again demurred: "It is not plausible that a burning passion and virtue long retain the same strength in a single heart. . . And if, against all appearances and custom, this combat between love and virtue were to last in her heart until the death of her husband, then she would be delighted to be able to bring love and virtue together by marrying a man of quality, the finest and most handsome gentleman of his time." Plausibility clings to the norm: it assumes and requires that human behavior conform to recognizable commonplaces (how long a woman's virtue lasts, for example). To behave implausibly is generally to refuse the social expectations that shape public opinion. Plausibility is one of the forms ideology takes in literature.

In the nineteenth-century, Stendhal, like Bussy but for different reasons, expressed his reservations about Lafayette's heroine. He thought Madame de Clèves made a mistake in turning down the man every woman at the court would have "been proud to call . . her lover" (4). The Princess of Clèves, he wrote in *On Love*, "should have said nothing to her husband, and given herself to Monsieur de Nemours." In the second place, he speculates: "If Madame de Clèves had lived to an advanced age and reached that period in which one reflects on life, and where the pleasures of pride appear in all their poverty, she would have regretted her decision. She would have wanted to live like Madame de Lafayette."

In a footnote, Stendhal turned to biography to explain what he meant by this comparison: "It is well known that this famous woman probably composed *The Princess of Clèves* in the company of Monsieur de la Rochefoucauld, and that the two authors spent the last twenty years of their life together in perfect friendship." Critics who read heroines as stand-ins for their authors have not served women writers well; by authorizing the anecdotes of their (love) lives, this kind of biographical criticism tends to undercut the authority and originality of their plots. It is perhaps for this reason that Lafayette as a woman writer published her novel unsigned. The withholding of authorial signature discourages readers from bringing judgments about the story of the author's life to bear on her literary creation.

The bookseller's notice that frames *The Princess of Clèves* states that the author of this story "remains anonymous that you may judge more freely and impartially the work's own merit." What do we know about Marie-Madeleine Pioche de la Vergne, Comtesse de Lafayette, the woman, that sheds light on her text? Very little, especially if one has in mind revelations for a *roman à clef.* Lafayette published two successful novels before *The Princess of Clèves, La Princess de Montpensier* in 1662 and *Zayde* in 1669; her other works, *Histoire de Mme. Henriette d'Angleterre, Mémoires de la Cour de France pour les années 1688 et 1689,* as well as her *nouvelle, La Comtesse de Tende,* were published posthumously. Unlike Madame de Clèves, she led a long and active life in Paris. Cordially separated from her husband, in charge of family affairs, she furthered the interests of her sons with such energy for litigation that her friend the Marquise de Sévigné described her as having "a hundred arms that reach everywhere." In her fashionable salon on the rue de Vaugirard, she talked about books (doubtless including her own) and analyzed the vagaries of social events with friends, intellectuals and leading literary lights, including—famously—La Rochefoucauld.

Lafayette cultivated connections and interests at the Court of Louis XIV; she was a frequent visitor at the Palais Royal and at Saint-Cloud. Her familiarity with the complexities and intrigues of contemporary court relationships—love affairs and political alliances—may well have provided living detail to her substantial knowledge of life in the glamorous French court a hundred years earlier. The historical detail seemed to matter to her. In a letter in which she plays literary critic to her own anonymous text, Lafayette emphasized the accuracy of *The Princess of Clèves*: "it's a perfect imitation of the world of the court and the way people live there. . . . In fact, it's not a novel: properly speaking, it's a memoir.

According to what I've heard, that originally was in the title of the book, but it was changed." But should we take this critic at her word?

Novel or memoir, what matters is the special quality of court life that powerfully frames and structures the love story: in Lafayette's court, affairs of the heart cannot be cleanly separated from affairs of state. In this atmosphere where "love was often mixed with politics and politics with love" and "pleasure and intrigue occupied everyone's attention" (12), falling in love is not a private matter. This is what the opening pages of the novel, with their flurry of genealogies and alliances, make clear.

Will the Duke of Nemours marry Queen Elizabeth? Our first encounter with the heroine of Lafayette's novel is set against that question of national interest. In the midst of these speculations, an extraordinarily beautiful young woman of sixteen, the character who will become the Princesse de Clèves, but who is now Mademoiselle de Chartres, is brought to the court by her mother. Madame de Chartres, who had raised her daughter alone after her husband's death, is now seeking a proper match for her only child. On the day after her arrival, Mademoiselle de Chartres goes alone to a court jeweler to find a match for some precious stones. While she is with the jeweler, the Prince de Clèves walks in and is stunned by the beauty of this unknown woman. He stares at her so unabashedly that Mademoiselle de Chartres, embarrassed by the insistency of his gaze, leaves abruptly. The prince is left wondering who she is and determined to find out.

The scene at the jeweler's is an emblem of the many ways life at the court constrains the princess. It establishes early in the novel a sequence of events that the plot repeats often, always with meaningful consequences: every gesture the princess makes is scrutinized and circumscribed by others who want to decipher her actions in their terms and place her in their story. She becomes, finally, a site in which others exercise their interpretive powers. Her resistance before their efforts to interpret her motives also figures the difficulty for readers of interpreting the novel itself.

When Mademoiselle de Chartres agrees to marry the man who fell madly in love with her at first sight, Madame de Chartres is overjoyed even though it is clear that her daughter is far from returning the prince's feelings: "she could marry him with less reluctance than she would feel in marrying anyone else, but . . . she did not feel any particular attraction to him" (18). The mother, who has come to the court in order to find a husband for her daughter in a world of political alliances, and who has been foiled in her plans by her enemies, is grateful to the Prince of Clèves for his suit and impresses her gratitude on her daughter. But her enthusiasm for this marriage doesn't square with her own maternal pedagogy: she had, after all, taught her daughter that given the "insincerity of men," and "the unhappiness in the home brought about by illicit love affairs," the only chance a woman has of being happy is to "love her husband and be loved by him" (8). In a court whose king himself is passionately and publicly devoted to a longstanding adulterous affair, what are we to make of the mother's lessons? Can we expect the princess to live happily ever after having realized only part of the mother's calculus: marriage to a man who loves her?

Shortly after the wedding ceremony, the princess attends a royal ball and meets the Duc de Nemours, a man described as "nature's masterpiece," and who awakens in her all the feelings her husband left dormant. Her mother silently observes the steady progress of this inclination and from her deathbed names the feelings her daughter has neither spoken of nor admitted to herself: "You are attracted to Monsieur de Nemours; I don't ask you to confess it." The mother's dying words urge her daughter to take whatever measures are required to keep herself from falling "to the level of other women" (39). The first part of the four-part novel ends with the twin facts of the mother's death and the daughter's desire. A maternal admonition echoes throughout the novel as the woman struggles to be both her mother's daughter and herself.

To her daughter's question about the king's passion for the Duchesse de Valentinois, Madame de Chartres replies with a maxim—"if you judge by appearances at court, you will always be deceived" (25)—and with an account of the king's affair. This narrative is the first of the embedded stories that punctuate and comment upon the princess's education and thus construct a text within a text. These stories, taken both from history and from current court intrigues, are not digressions from the main lines of the plot but examples that point to a moral; they present the consequences of the mutual determination of passion and politics in the fabric of court life. When Monsieur de Clèves tells his wife the story of Madame de Tournon's betrayal of his friend the Comte de Sancerre, the connection between the anecdote and the main plot are exceptionally clear: "If my mistress, or even my wife," the prince quotes himself as saying to his friend, "should sincerely and frankly confess that she loved another, I would be pained but not embittered. I would stop being her lover, or her husband, as the case might be, in order to help her and to sympathize with her" (45). The princess makes the connection, but doesn't take up her husband's offer until the third part of the novel when, overwhelmed by her feelings and pressed to explain herself, she finally tells him what he thinks he wants to know. Madame de Clèves, however, unlike the duplicitous Madame de Tournon, is not confessing her guilt but declaring her innocence; this is part of what leads her to say that her declaration was made not "out of weakness but courage." The Prince of Clèves, in many ways as exceptional as his wife, recognizes the magnitude of that gesture: "you have made me unhappy," he observes, "by the greatest proof of fidelity that a woman could ever

give to her husband" (99). But is the prince able to
follow his own advice and overcome the jealousy of a
husband in order to help his wife? Like the mother who
wanted her daughter to regard her not as a mother, but
"as a friend . . . to confide in . . . about these affairs of
the heart" (13), the husband says he values "sincerity
above everything else" (45). *Can a mother love as a
friend? Can a husband love as a mother?*

As we saw earlier, this scene in which a wife admits to
her husband her passionate feelings for another man
captured the imagination of seventeenth-century readers
of *The Princess of Clèves*, who heatedly argued for and
against its novelistic validity. One of the most remarkable
features of the novel is that it rehearsed its readers'
reactions in the text itself. Overheard and repeated as
gossip, the confession as a story is evaluated within the
novel for its plausibility; it even comes back to the princess as a story that she herself doesn't find credible. The
power of this scene, then, is not uniquely a function of
the unlikely exchange it stages between a husband and a
wife. It is also powerful because within the fiction it
becomes an object lesson on the nature of gender and
narrative.

It seems somehow inevitable that this intensely private
avowal be overheard and that the man who overhears the
princess confess that she loves another man is the man the
princess loves. Hidden from view in an alcove within
their pavilion, Nemours hears all and then tells all: "unable to contain his amazement at what Madame de Clèves
had done, he told the story to the vidame" (102). In this
universe where everything is seen, made known, recounted
and interpreted, the princess's confession, like the woman's love letter that falls from the Vidame de Chartres's
pocket, circulates. Designed to protect the princess from
betraying her feelings for Nemours, her avowal turns out
to make her more vulnerable to exposure. Monsieur de
Clèves pleads abjectly to learn the name of the man who

has found the way to touch the heart of the woman he himself had failed to move, and makes himself sick trying to find out. Like the husband, Nemours wants the wife to say the lover's name; and like the husband, the lover finds himself both happy and unhappy: "this same conversation, which had just revealed her love for him, also convinced him that he would never receive any outward indication of it" (101). Thus, through a paradoxical effect of gender arrangements, the husband and lover find themselves aligned together *as men* over the question of a woman's desire, and what they desperately want to find out is precisely what she passionately resolves to withhold.

The structure of the confession is repeated in an equally disturbing enactment of triangulated desire that takes place in the last book of the novel. Here, as in the scene at the jeweler's, the princess sets out alone to satisfy a desire of her own. She leaves the court for the house at Coulommiers without her husband and takes with her paintings that represent scenes of distinguished action in recent French history. The portraits of the participants, the narrator points out, were strikingly faithful, and in a rare moment of discursive coyness, we are told that it was *perhaps* Monsieur de Nemours's presence in these scenes that made Madame de Clèves want the paintings with her.

In a scene that is justly famous, the princess sits alone late at night in the pavilion of her country estate winding ribbons around a walking stick belonging to Nemours, the man she has come to Coulommiers to avoid. When she finishes her handiwork, she picks up a candle and goes over to gaze lovingly at Nemours's portrait in the painting of the siege of Metz. The sexual symbolism of this scene has not been lost on post-Freudian critics. But what seems at least as important as the princess's gestures of sublimated desire is the fact that like the confession to her husband the expression of her desire is again witnessed, that again the witness is the Duc de Nemours,

peering into Madame de Clèves' windows from behind a
fence. The voyeurism here is even more complex than in
the confession, for Nemours himself is secretly observed
by a servant dispatched by the princess's anxious husband. Once more the husband and the lover are bound to
and against each other over the spectacle of a woman's
pleasure. As in the first episode in the garden, the lover
is both gratified by the evidence of the woman's desire
and mystified by her determination to conceal what she
feels: "How can I be loved by Madame de Clèves and
still feel miserable?" (136) Despite Nemours's frustra-
tion, when the servant reports to the Prince de Clèves
that his rival spent the night in the forest garden, the
husband can only imagine that the duke and the princess
spent it together. He no longer believes his wife's virtue
had the strength of her confession.

*Should a virtuous woman tell her husband she is in love
with another man?* Or putting the question another way:
what happens in a novel when a character performs an
action everyone—including herself—finds incredible? What
happens *to* a novel whose plot unfolds from its implausi-
bility? The final scenes of the novel repeat its opening
moves with classically pointed symmetry: the princess's
errand to a neighborhood merchant to buy some ornamental silk recalls her visit to the jeweler's; the meeting
between Nemours and the princess at the vidame's house
where these two remarkable beings speak of their desire
to each other openly for the first time replays their dancing together at the ball without having been introduced.
The symmetry of these scenes brings us back to the
question of the marriage plot with which the princess's
story opened.

If seventeenth-century readers were mainly preoccupied with the advisability of confiding in one's husband,
readers today are more troubled by the princess's decision not to marry Nemours after her husband's death.

Like Bussy and Stendhal, many think she has missed her chance at happiness. How does this decision, which is still an object of critical debate today, come about? The death of Monsieur de Clèves of course weighs heavily in the economy of the novel's ending; the princess holds herself responsible for her husband's death and blames herself for not loving him as he had loved her. She hears the voice of duty speak to her in the tones of her mother's voice and invokes her peace of mind, that seventeenth-century concept of "repos" so difficult to translate: "repos" is not a passive state of restfulness—repose—but an active process of self-mastery.

In the mourning period after her husband's death, the princess thinks her passion for Nemours has died, but when she finally sees him again, she discovers that her love is still very much alive. From her window she catches a glimpse of him, and pictures him "gazing upon the walls that enclosed her" (147); her love instantly comes rushing back to overwhelm her and remove all the obstacles to their union. To the extent that she sees Nemours as someone *like* her (not like other men as she is not like other women), she allows herself to imagine marriage. But as she finally admits her love *to* him, she returns to her earlier anxieties about the rules that govern the relations between the sexes in her world: "But do men in marriage remain forever in love? Ought I to hope for a miracle in my case? Can I put myself in a situation to watch this love upon which all my happiness depends come to an end?" (154)

In Lafayette's universe, one doesn't choose one's desire, but the story through which one lives it is another matter. In love but choosing not to marry the man she is in love with, the princess refuses to resemble either the "other women" her mother invoked or the heroines of other novels against which the critics judged her. The Princess of Clèves chooses instead a life spent—a little like Persephone's in its oscillation between two places—both in the convent and at home. Beyond marriage and

finally beyond interpretation, the princess withdraws from
sight, but not perhaps from happiness.

Since the publication of the first Signet Classic edition
of Lafayette's novel in 1961, feminism has vastly compli-
cated our thinking about the relations between gender
and culture, especially about the place of women's writing in the republic of letters. This has also meant learning
to read women's writing for what it might have to tell us
about the representation of gender itself. In her final
scene with Nemours, the princess says in a voice resonant
with pleasure: "in the end this confession will have no
consequences" (152). We have only begun to take the
measure of that claim.

BOOKSELLER TO READER

Whatever approbation this story might have merited upon our several readings of it, the author would not consent to affix his name to it, lest his name might in some way reduce the possibility of the book's success. He knows from experience that we sometimes condemn works on the mean opinion we have of their authors, and he knows, too, that an author's reputation often enhances the value of his books. So he remains anonymous that you may judge more freely and impartially on the work's own merits whether it is as pleasing to the public's taste as I hope it will be.

BOOK I

❦

Opulence and gallantry were never so brilliantly displayed in France as they were in the last years of Henri II's reign. He was a chivalrous king, handsome, and in love. Although his passion for Diane de Poitiers, Duchesse de Valentinois, had begun more than twenty years before, it was now no less intense, nor were the tokens of his passionate love less dazzling. He was a great sportsman, and much of his time was devoted to physical exercise. Every day there were hunting, tennis, ballets, tilting at the ring, or some other such sportive diversions. Madame de Valentinois' colors and banners were everywhere visible. She herself was present too, dressed in finery, which would have been more appropriate to the tastes of her young granddaughter, Mademoiselle de La Marck, who was then of marriageable age.

The presence of the queen was her justification for being there. Catherine de Médicis was still a beautiful princess though no longer in her first youth. She loved pomp, opulence, and pleasure. The king had married her when he was still the Duc d'Orléans before the death of his older brother, the dauphin—who at that time was destined to reign on the throne of France.

Catherine de Médicis, by nature ambitious, took great delight in her reign. It seemed she did not mind at all the king's amorous attachment to the Duchesse de Valentinois, and, for certain, she gave no sign of being jealous of the

I

duchess. But then too, it must be said, she was such a good pretender it was difficult to judge her real thoughts. Besides, strategy dictated that she keep this duchess close by her in order to insure the presence of the king.

The king loved the company of women, even those with whom he was not in love: every day he betook himself to the queen's apartment at that hour when he knew the most beautiful and the most elegant of both sexes would be present.

Never was there a court with so many beautiful ladies and handsome men; it seemed that nature was taking great delight in showing off the favors that she had so profusely lavished upon these princes and princesses.

Madame Élisabeth de France, who later became the Queen of Spain, had begun to reveal an exceptional mind and to show that incomparable beauty which was to be so fatal to her in the end. Marie Stuart, Queen of Scotland, who had just married the dauphin François de Valois and whom everyone referred to as the queen-dauphine, was, in mind and body, a perfect delight. She had been reared at the court of France and reflected all its elegance and urbanity. She was born with such refined taste for beauty that, despite her youthful years, she cared for and knew more about elegance than anybody. The queen her mother-in-law and Madame the king's sister also loved poetry, the theater, and music. François I had made the arts fashionable; the taste for them still remained so in France. And since the king, his son, liked physical exercises so much, there was every kind of pleasure to be found at court. But what added more to its elegance and splendor was the constant attendance there, in great numbers, of princes and highborn noblemen. All these—and I will name them—were, in different ways, the adornment and admiration of their century.

The King of Navarre was revered by all, not only for his exalted rank, but for the loftiness of his character as well. He was an excellent soldier, even a rival to the great Duc de Guise, who, on many occasions and in the most perilous situations, used to let the king take his place as general of the armies, and fight beside him as a common soldier. This duke had distinguished himself so valorously and so successfully that there was indeed no captain in the army who did not look upon him a bit enviously. And bravery was only one of a great number of his fine qualities: his mind was sharp; his knowledge broad; his soul noble and refined; his talent in politics as eminent as his ability on the field of battle. The Cardinal de Lorraine, his brother, was inordinately ambitious, learned, and eloquent. He had acquired a profound knowledge that he put to good service—and to his own advantage—in defending the Catholic Church, which was at that time coming under severe attack. The Chevalier de Guise, later known as the grand prior, was a prince admired by everyone—a man of distinction: intelligent, clever, and celebrated all over Europe for his courage. The Prince de Condé, small and ugly but possessed of a proud and haughty soul, charmed the most beautiful women with his engaging wit. The Duc de Nevers, in spite of his age, was the delight of the court. He had won a fabulous reputation in warfare and in other exploits of high adventure. This duke had three sons; but it was the second, the Prince de Clèves, who had all those qualities of character worthy of upholding the luster of the family name. He was brave, magnanimous, and, for all his young years, prudent to a remarkable degree.

The Vidame de Chartres, descendant of the ancient family of Vendôme, whose name even the princes of blood did not disdain, was pre-eminent in the arts of war and love. He was handsome, prepossessing in appearance, spirited, bold, and generous. All these fine qualities in him were vital, dazzling, and quite in evidence. If anyone could be said to be worthy of comparison with the Duc de Nemours, it would be he.

The Duc de Nemours was nature's masterpiece among men. The very least that could be said of him was that he was the most handsome at court. But what really set him

apart from all others was a certain distinction and charm
of mind, appearance, and deportment that was his own
special hallmark. Both men and women were fascinated
by his engaging personality. He displayed extraordinary
dexterity in everything he did. Even about his manner of
dressing, there was something that begged you to imitate
but that was in fact inimitable—in a word there was a
certain style about his person which made it impossible to
take your eyes off him whenever he was in the room.
There was not a lady at court who would not have been
proud to have called him her lover. Few on whom he did
bestow his attentions could boast of having resisted his
charm. Indeed, many to whom he had given no signs of
affection loved him unrequitedly. By nature he was so
gentle and gallant that it was impossible for him to be
totally indifferent to any who tried to please him. For this
reason he had several mistresses, but it was extremely
difficult to guess who it was whom he really loved. He
was often in the company of the queen-dauphine, whose
beauty, kindness, and concern for everyone's well-being—
but more especially because of her forward concern for
him—would lead you to believe that his love was for her.

Her uncles, the Messieurs de Guise, had gained in
prestige and esteem at court through her marriage. They
sought equality with the princes of blood and ambitiously
wanted to share the same power and privileges as the
Connétable de Montmorency, who, in fact, administered
the government for the king. The Duc de Guise and the
Maréchal de Saint-André were the king's favorites. But
whether people were drawn to his majesty the king out of
kindness or business interest, they could only maintain
their position by deferring to the Duchesse de Valentinois,
who, although she was no longer either young or beautiful, governed the king so absolutely that one could say
she was both mistress of his person and of his kingdom.

The king had always been fond of the constable, and,
as soon as he had become king, he brought him back
from exile where François the First had sent him.

The court was divided: some supported the Messieurs de Guise; and others favored the constable, who had on his side the princes of blood. Both factions sought, however, to enlist the support of the Duchesse de Valentinois. The Duc d'Aumale, brother of the Duc de Guise, had married one of her daughters, and the constable wanted to make this same match. He was not satisfied with having married his oldest son to Madame Diane, daughter of the king by a Piedmontese lady who had gone into a convent as soon as she gave birth to her child. This marriage had been difficult to arrange because of certain indiscreet promises Monsieur de Montmorency had made to Mademoiselle de Piennes, one of the queen's attendants. Although the king had overcome all these embarrassing obstacles with extreme tact and kindness, the constable did not feel quite secure with Madame de Valentinois so long as he could not detach her from the Messieurs de Guise.

Madame de Valentinois herself was beginning to feel uncomfortable because of the rising importance of the Messieurs de Guise. She had put off as long as she could the marriage of the dauphin to the Queen of Scotland. The beauty and unusual intelligence of this young queen, and the nobility which this marriage would certainly afford to the Messieurs de Guise, were unbearable to her. She especially detested the Cardinal de Lorraine, who had too often spoken sarcastically to her, even condescendingly, and it did appear to her that he was taking sides with the queen. At this time the constable found the Duchesse de Valentinois kindly disposed toward him and inclined to arrange a marriage between her granddaughter, Mademoiselle de La Marck, and his second son, Monsieur d'Anville, who, later, during the reign of Charles the Ninth succeeded to his office. The connétable never imagined that Monsieur d'Anville would oppose this marriage, as Monsieur de Montmorency had his, but so it was, and for reasons that were not disclosed to him. Monsieur d'Anville was passionately in love with the queen-dauphine, and though he held little hope in the way of a successful outcome of this love affair, he was determined not to enter upon an engagement that might compromise his interests.

The Maréchal de Saint-André was the only person at court who had not taken sides. He was a favorite. The king had liked him ever since he was dauphin, and had made him a marshal of France at an age when it was unusual to receive any high honors at all. But he maintained his prestige at court by virtue of his own superiority and charm, the excellence of his table, the taste with which his house was furnished, and by a liberality such as few could afford—all made possible by the king's generosity.

The king was prodigal with those he loved; though not perfect, he had many fine attributes. He especially liked war and was highly skillful at it. If one excluded the battle of Saint-Quentin, his reign had been one victory after another. He had personally won the battle of Renti, had conquered Piedmont, and routed the English from France. He saw the tide change against Charles Quint outside the town of Metz which this king was vainly besieging with all the forces of the empire and of Spain. Nevertheless, the disaster at Saint-Quentin had lessened the chances of victory, and since the spoils of war seemed now equally divided between the two kings, they were ready to consider peace.

The dowager Duchesse de Lorraine had begun to make overtures of peace at the time of the dauphin's marriage. Ever since, secret negotiations had been going on. Finally, Cercamp in the Artois region was selected as the meeting place. The Cardinal de Lorraine, the Connétable de Montmorency, and the Maréchal de Saint-André were the representatives of the king. The Duke of Alba and the Prince of Orange represented Philip the Second, and the Duc and Duchesse de Lorraine were the mediators. The principal articles concerned the marriage of Madame Élisabeth of France with don Carlos, Infante of Spain, and the marriage of Madame the king's sister with the Duc de Savoie.

The king, however, stayed at the frontier, and it was there he received news about the death of Mary Queen of England. He sent the Comte de Randan to Elizabeth to congratulate her on the eventuality of her succession to the throne. She received him warmly; since her rights were not yet too firmly established, it was advantageous to be recognized by the King of France. The count found her to be well versed in the ways of the French court. She was well informed about the personalities who gathered there. But especially she had heard all about the Duc de Nemours. In fact, she spoke to the count about this duke so often and so eagerly that when Monsieur de Randan on his return reported to the king about his trip, he told the king there was nothing that Monsieur de Nemours could not have from this queen but for the asking. And furthermore, he did not doubt that Monsieur de Nemours could marry her if she so wished. That very evening the king spoke to the duke about it, making the count detail the entire conversation he had had with Elizabeth. He counseled the duke to go and try his luck. At first Monsieur de Nemours did not think that the king was serious, but when he saw then, on the contrary, that he was.

"At least, Sire," he said, "if I should embark on such a fanciful venture, on your advice and for the service of your majesty, I should beg you to keep it all a secret until the success of this venture has been vindicated in the eyes of the public. Otherwise, it would appear that I am a vain man, indeed, to suppose that a queen, who has never even met me, could wish to marry me for love."

The king promised that he would speak to no one but the constable about their plan. In fact, he was of the opinion that secrecy was absolutely essential for its success. Monsieur de Randan advised the Duc de Nemours to go to England on some simple pretext as a traveler, but the duke could not agree to this. He would send Lignerolles, a man of some intelligence and his favorite friend, to

sound out the feelings of the queen and to try to effect
some relationship.

While awaiting the outcome of this commission, the
king went to call on the Duc de Savoie, who was then in
Brussels with the King of Spain. The death of Mary
Tudor had brought many obstacles to the peace; so the
conference broke up at the end of November and the
king returned to Paris.

At this time there arrived on the scene a beauty who
attracted the eyes of everyone at court. She was a para-
gon of beauty. Indeed she must have been, since she
drew the attention of all in a place where lovely women
were the rule. She was of the same family as the Vidame
de Chartres and was one of the greatest heiresses in
France. Her father had died a young man, and had left
her to be brought up by his widow, Madame de Chartres,
a wealthy, virtuous, and noble lady. After her husband's
death, she had left the court for many years to devote
herself entirely to her daughter's education, cultivating
not only her mind and caring for her beauty, but also
trying to make her virtuous and good. Most mothers,
overly protective, think it is wrong ever to speak of love
to their daughters. But not so Madame de Chartres! She
often described it to her daughter; she would show her
what was most charming about it, so that more persua-
sively she might teach her its dangers. She told her of the
insincerity of men, of their deceitful ways, of their infidelity. She spoke of the unhappiness in the home brought
about by illicit love affairs. And then, on the other hand,
she described how peaceful, upright, honest ladies were,
how beauty and birth, wedded to a virtuous life, gave
fragrance, bloom, and distinction to one's person. She
made her daughter see also that virtue must be won by
extreme wariness and by clinging to the only thing that
can bring happiness to a woman—which is, to love her
husband and to be loved by him.

This heiress belonged to one of the really great families

of France. Although she was extremely young, she had
already received many proposals of marriage. Madame
de Chartres, who was an extremely proud woman, could
find no one worthy of her daughter. When the girl was
sixteen, Madame de Chartres decided to take her to
court. As soon as she was presented, the vidame went to
meet her. He was enchanted by Mademoiselle de Chartres'
great beauty—and well he might be. She was absolutely
ravishing. Her fair complexion, her honey-blonde hair,
her classical features, her poise—all radiated grace and
charm.

On the day following her arrival, she went to match
some precious stones at the jewelry store of an Italian
who did a world-wide trade. This man had come from
Florence with the queen and had become so rich by his
business transactions that he lived more like a grand
duke than a merchant. While she was there, the Prince
de Clèves arrived. He was so taken by Mademoiselle de
Chartres' beauty that he could scarcely hide his admiration. And Mademoiselle de Chartres could not help blush-
ing, noticing the state into which she had thrown him.
However, she quickly regained her composure, and paid
no more attention to the behavior of this prince than was
required by ordinary rules of etiquette to such a distin-
guished-looking man. Monsieur de Clèves gazed at her
with admiration, unable to comprehend this phenomenon
of beauty whom he did not recognize. He deduced by her
air and deportment that she must certainly be a lady of
high birth. Her youthfulness made him believe that she
was unmarried, but not seeing her mother, and hearing
the Italian, who did not know her either, call her "Madame," he did not know what to think. He continued to
stare, and, whereas most young girls enjoy seeing the
pleasure their beauty effects upon others, he noticed his
glances embarrassed her. He felt that he was the cause of
her apparent impatience to leave. Indeed, she did leave
soon afterward. Monsieur de Clèves consoled himself
when she was out of sight with the hope of finding out

who she was, but, much to his surprise, no one seemed to
know. He remained impressed by her beauty and by the
modesty noticeable in all her actions. One can say that
from that moment he was madly in love with her. He
went that evening to see Madame the king's sister.

This princess was universally respected by virtue of the
powerful influence she exercised over the king her
brother—an influence so great that the king, when making peace, had consented to yield the duchy of Piedmont
so that she could marry the Duc de Savoie. Although she
had long wanted to be married, she would never settle
for anyone but a sovereign, and, for this reason, she had
refused to marry the King of Navarre when he was the
Duc de Vendôme. She had wanted to marry the Duc de
Savoie ever since she had spotted him at Nice during a
conclave between François the First and Pope Paul the
Third. Because she was a clever woman and artistically
inclined, she attracted the very best people. At certain
hours of the day, the entire court was entertained in her
apartment. Monsieur de Clèves was usually present. He
was so impressed by the charm and beauty of Mademoiselle de Chartres that scarcely could he talk of anything
else. He told all about his adventure and never tired of
singing the praises of this unknown lady whom he had
seen. Madame assured him that no such person of his
description existed since, if she did, everyone would know
of her. Madame de Dampierre, her lady-in-waiting and a
friend of Madame de Chartres, overhearing this conversation, whispered to the Madame that this person whom
Monsieur de Clèves had seen undoubtedly was Mademoiselle de Chartres. Madame turned to him and said that if
he would come back the next day she would see to it that
he met this beauty who had impressed him so much.

Indeed, on the following day, Mademoiselle de Chartres
did make an appearance. She was received by the queens
with the greatest kindness imaginable and with such admiration that she heard nothing but whispered praises
from all quarters. She received these praises quite mod-

estly, appearing to take no notice of them, or, at least, giving no indication that she was touched by them. Then she went to Madame's apartment. Madame, after complimenting Mademoiselle de Chartres on her beauty, told her of the effect she had had upon Monsieur de Clèves. A moment later, he entered.

"Come in," Madame said to him. "See if I have not kept my word. Is not this the beautiful lady you were looking for? You may thank me, for I have already told her how much you admire her."

Monsieur de Clèves was overjoyed to see this person whom he found so attractive was of a family name in keeping with her beauty. He went over to her and begged her not to forget that he was the first to admire her, and that, without knowing who she was, it was he who had the most respect and esteem for her.

The Chevalier de Guise and Monsieur de Clèves left Madame's apartment together. At first they talked of nothing but Mademoiselle de Chartres. Then they thought that they were exaggerating too much her beauty and charm, so they stopped talking about her. But on the days that followed, whenever they met, this new beauty at court was for a long time the subject of all their conversations.

The queen was very fond of her too and extended to her the utmost respect. The queen-dauphine made her one of her favorites and asked Madame de Chartres to bring her daughter frequently to see her. The king's daughters often sent for her to take part in their amusements. Indeed, she was loved and admired by the whole court—with the sole exception of Madame de Valentinois. It was not her beauty that was especially disturbing to Madame de Valentinois: long experience taught her that, so far as the king was concerned, there was nothing to fear, but she hated the Vidame de Chartres. She had hoped to win him to her side through the marriage of one of his daughters, but he had preferred to align himself with the queen. Therefore, now madame could not look with favor upon

a person who bore the De Chartres name and upon
whom he apparently lavished affection.

The Prince de Clèves now was madly in love with
Mademoiselle de Chartres and he longed to marry her.
But he feared that Madame de Chartres herself was too
proud to marry off her daughter to any man excepting
the oldest of the house. However, his family was so noble
(the Comte d'Eu, the oldest, had just married a person
very nearly of royal blood) that the fears of Monsieur de
Clèves on this issue stemmed from the fact that he was in
love rather than from legitimate reasons. He had many
rivals, of whom the most formidable seemed to be the
Chevalier de Guise on account of his birth, his qualities,
and the high repute of his family. The Chevalier de Guise
had fallen in love with Mademoiselle de Chartres that
very first day he saw her. Now both the prince and the
chevalier knew of each other's feelings toward the mademoiselle. Although they had been friends, their friendship now cooled somewhat. Monsieur de Clèves still
hoped he had the advantage over most of his rivals
since he had seen her first. He felt this was a good omen.
But he anticipated difficulties with his father, the Duc de
Nevers, who was on intimate terms with the Duchesse de
Valentinois. Since she was the sworn enemy of the Vidame
de Chartres, this was reason enough for the Duc de
Nevers to block the marriage of his son to the vidame's
niece.

Madame de Chartres, who had very carefully tried to
inculcate in her daughter stern principles of virtue, continued to advance the same precautions in a place where
there were so many instances of danger and where these
precautions were so necessary. Ambition and gallantry
were the soul of the court and consumed alike the ener-
gies of both men and women. There were so many intrigues, so many different cliques, and the women were
so involved in them, that love was often mixed with
politics and politics with love. No one was calm or indifferent: everyone was taken up with the business of ad-

vancing his own position by pleasing, by serving, or by harming someone else. Boredom and idleness were unknown. Pleasure and intrigue occupied everyone's attention. The ladies attached themselves to the queen, the queen-dauphine, the Queen of Navarre, Madame the king's sister, or the Duchesse de Valentinois. These attachments were made purely on the basis of inclination, self-interest, or whim. Those who were young and professed a certain puritanism leagued themselves with the queen; those who were young and in search of pleasure and love courted the queen-dauphine. The Queen of Navarre had her favorites; she was young and exercised much power over her husband, the King of Navarre: he was close to the constable, and for this reason, very influential. Madame the king's sister was still beautiful, and she attracted several ladies to her side. The Duchesse de Valentinois chose a few of those ladies to be close friends of hers because their dispositions matched her own. She entertained them only on those days when it amused her to hold court like the queen.

All these different cliques vied with one another. The ladies of one were jealous of those who made up the cliques of the other; all competed for favors or lovers. Reputation and high position were linked to less important interests, but no less feverishly sought after. Thus, there was a sort of ordered agitation at court, which made it all quite pleasant, but also precarious, for a young lady. Madame de Chartres was aware of this danger and thought only of means of guarding her daughter against them. She asked her, not as a mother but as a friend, to confide in her about these affairs of heart, promising to help and guide her in these matters that could often be troublesome to a young girl.

The Chevalier de Guise made his feelings for and his intentions toward Mademoiselle de Chartres so apparent that everyone knew of them. However he saw immediately the impossibility of such a marriage. He knew well that he was not at all a suitable match for Mademoiselle

de Chartres, since he had little wealth to support his
rank. Furthermore, his brothers would not approve of
any marriage for him, for fear of abasing the prestige of
the family name (which the marriage of the younger ones
generally did). The Cardinal de Lorraine was quick to
point out to his brother, the chevalier, that he was not
mistaken. The cardinal absolutely forbade this attachment his brother had for Mademoiselle de Chartres, but
did not offer any really valid reasons. The cardinal nursed
a secret hate for the vidame which later was made public.
Therefore, to any other marriage but this one, the cardinal would have gladly consented. He said publicly how
much he was opposed to such an arrangement. Consequently, Madame de Chartres was not a little hurt. She
took great pains to point out that the cardinal really had
nothing at all to fear since she would never even consider
such a marriage. The vidame did the same. More than
Madame de Chartres, he felt hurt because he knew the
reasons for the cardinal's position.

The Prince de Clèves, like the Chevalier de Guise, also
had unmasked to all at court his love for Mademoiselle
de Chartres. The Duc de Nevers learned of this attachment with annoyance; but he believed he had only to
speak to his son to make him change his mind. He was
greatly surprised, however, to find that his son had intentions of marrying this Mademoiselle de Chartres. He
reprimanded his son and flew into such a rage over his
son's intentions that the story quickly spread to the court—
and even to Madame de Chartres. It had never occurred
to her for a moment that Monsieur de Nevers would
regard this marriage with her daughter other than as a
distinct advantage for his son. And she was most surprised that the houses of Clèves and Guise, instead of
wishing for such an alliance, should fear it. She was so
enraged that now she was determined to marry her daughter to someone who would rank above those who considered themselves so proudly superior to her.

After a little reflection, she decided upon the prince-dauphin, son of the Duc de Montpensier. At court there was no one grander than he. Madame de Chartres was a clever woman. Aided by the influence of the vidame and encouraged indeed by the fact that her daughter was an heiress of considerable means, she maneuvered so adroitly that Monsieur de Montpensier seemed indeed to favor this marriage. And it did appear that there would be no serious difficulties in the way of this alliance.

The vidame had a scheme: he knew that Monsieur d'Anville, a close friend of the Prince de Montpensier, was in love with the queen-dauphine and that she exercised a tremendous influence over him. So he decided to enlist her help in advancing the cause of Mademoiselle de Chartres with the king and the prince. He spoke to the queen about this. She was delighted with the plan, since it concerned the advancement of Mademoiselle de Chartres whom she liked very much. She told the vidame, however, that this would not rest too pleasantly with the Cardinal de Lorraine, her uncle. But she assured him she would overlook this detail since the cardinal was always taking the queen's side against her.

Young ladies in love are always glad to find some pretext of talking to those who are in love with them. As soon as the vidame left, Madame la Dauphine ordered Châtelart, a close friend of Monsieur d'Anville, and well aware of Monsieur d'Anville's love for her, to tell him that he should go to the queen's apartment that evening. Châtelart gladly and respectfully did her bidding. This gentleman, who came from a good family in the Dauphiné, rose above his family by his own qualities and talents. He was received and well treated at court by all the great noblemen, and was especially attached to Monsieur d'Anville through the kindness of the house of Montmorency. He was handsome and adept in sports; he sang pleasantly, wrote poetry, and had a romantic side to him that so much pleased Monsieur d'Anville that Monsieur d'Anville confided to him the love he had for the queen-dauphine. This confidence brought Châtelart into frequent

contact with this princess. Seeing her so often, unfortunately, Châtelart fell in love with her, and this eventually
cost him his reason, and finally his life. Monsieur d'Anville did not fail to be at the queen's that evening. He
was very happy that he could be of some service to
Madame la Dauphine, and he promised to do all that she
wished. But Madame de Valentinois, having been ap-
prised of this intended marriage, so carefully thwarted its
possibilities by prejudicing the king against it that when
Monsieur d'Anville spoke to him about it, the king made
it very clear that he would not approve this marriage. He
even ordered Monsieur d'Anville to make these sentiments known to the Prince de Montpensier.

You can imagine how Madame de Chartres must have
felt when all her careful planning failed miserably. Her
enemies had won; her daughter had lost an advantage.

The queen-dauphine told Mademoiselle de Chartres
very kindly that she was sorry not to have been more
helpful.

"You see," she said, "my influence at court is slight.
The Duchesse de Valentinois and the queen hate me so,
that, either because of them or their followers, I never
can get what I want. And, really, I have done nothing
but try to please them. They hate me because my mother
the queen a long time ago made them jealous and suspicious. The king had been in love with my mother before
he loved Madame de Valentinois. And during the early
years of his marriage, before he had any children, though
in love with this Duchesse de Valentinois, he seemed
fanatically determined to get a divorce and marry the
queen my mother. Madame de Valentinois, who was
afraid of this very beautiful and clever woman whom he
had already loved, joined with the constable, who also
did not wish the king to marry a sister of the Messieurs
de Guise. They won the favor of the late king, and
though he mortally hated the Duchesse de Valentinois,
he did like his daughter-in-law the queen, so he worked
with them to prevent the king from divorcing her. But to

scended the bounds of ordinary respect and gratitude. Nor could he delude himself that she was hiding some deeper feeling, because, had there been any such, her extreme modesty would not, since they were engaged, have prevented her from revealing it. Hardly a day passed that he did not register his complaints to her.

"Can it be possible," he said, "that, now that I am to marry you, I could be unhappy? Yet, it is so. I am not happy. You only feel for me a sort of kindness which cannot satisfy me. You have neither the excitement nor the anxiety of love. Nor have you any of the afflictions of love. You are no more affected by my passion than you would be by an attachment that was only founded on the advantages of your wealth and not on the charms of your person."

"You are most unkind," she replied to him. "I don't know what more you can expect of me. It seems to me that propriety does not permit me to do much more than I have already done."

"True," he replied. "Outwardly you do appear to love me, and for this I would be extremely happy if only there was hidden something deeper. I also get the impression that instead of propriety holding you back, it is for reasons of propriety that you act at all. I do not move your affections nor touch your heart, and my presence causes you neither pleasure nor any other discomfort."

"You certainly cannot doubt," she said, "that being with you gives me joy. Surely you have remarked how I blush when you are near me."

"My dear, I am not deceived by your blushes," he answered. "They are symbols of your modesty and not indications of your love. I derive only what satisfaction I may from them."

Mademoiselle de Chartres did not know what to say in reply. All these subtle nuances were beyond her comprehension. Monsieur de Clèves saw only too well that she was a stranger to him, that her genuine feelings—really not understood by herself—were anything but satisfactory to him.

The Chevalier de Guise returned from a trip a few days before the wedding. Though he had given up hope of ever marrying Mademoiselle de Chartres himself because of the many insurmountable obstacles, he was, nonetheless, very much grieved to see her become the wife of another. This hurt did not extinguish his love for her. He was as madly in love with her as before. Mademoiselle de Chartres was well aware of his feelings. And he made it known to her that since he had come back, she was the cause of his unhappy state. He was so good and so charming that it was difficult not to feel sorry for him. She did pity him, but this was the extent of her emotion, and she told her mother so.

Madame de Chartres marveled at her daughter's candor, and for good reason. No one ever had a more frank and open disposition. But she was no less astonished that the girl's heart was untouched by the Prince of Cleves, especially as she saw only too well that it was untouched by any of the others. That was the reason she took great care in arranging this marriage with Monsieur de Clèves, impressing upon her daughter what she owed this man who had loved her before he even knew her. He had given ample testimony of his passion by preferring her to all others at a time when no one else dared think of her.

The marriage was performed. The ceremony took place in the Louvre, and in the evening the king, the queens, and the entire court attended a magnificent reception given by Madame de Chartres. The Chevalier de Guise dared not make himself conspicuous by staying away from this affair. So he was there, but so little master of his melancholy that everyone noticed his misery.

Monsieur de Clèves did not find that Mademoiselle de Chartres had changed her feelings by changing her name. His status as husband gave him new privileges but no new place in his wife's heart. Wanting always something more than mere possession as her husband, he did not

fail in his duties as a lover. Although she lived perfectly
well with him, he was not happy. His violent love, his
agitated heart, marred his joy. It was not a question of
jealousy. No husband was less suspicious of his wife, no
wife ever gave less cause for suspicion. She went every
day to the two queens and to Madame. She entertained a
host of young handsome men in her apartment, and was
entertained by the Duc de Nevers, her brother-in-law,
whose house was open to everybody. But she had a
certain air which commanded respect and which was so
far from being flirtatious that even the Maréchal de Saint-
André—a forward man and, what is more, a favorite of
the king—was moved by her beauty and dared not let it
be known. He was attentive and polite, but that was as
far as he went. Several others felt the same way. Madame de Chartres further instructed her daughter to be
most proper in her conduct so that the young Madame
De Clèves did project the image of being indeed unat-
tainable.

The Duchesse de Lorraine, while working for the peace,
had also "worked," in the meantime, a marriage for her
son, the Duc de Lorraine. It had been arranged with
Madame Claude de France, second daughter of the king.
The wedding was set for February.

In the meanwhile, the Duc de Nemours was living in
Brussels, entirely preoccupied with his English plans. He
passed his time receiving and sending messengers. His
hopes rose day by day, and at last, Lignerolles told him
that it was now time for the duke to go to England in
person and conclude the matter that had begun so well.
The Duc de Nemours was overjoyed at this bit of news,
as any young, ambitious man would have been, seeing
himself being carried to the throne by sheer dint of his
reputation. Though at first he had thought the whole
project impossible and fraught with too many difficulties,
now, imperceptibly, he was adjusting to its inevitability.

He sent orders to Paris with all speed to have an
elaborate retinue so that he might make his appearance

at the English court with all suitable brilliance. Then he hastened to Paris to attend the marriage of the Duc de Lorraine.

He arrived on the eve of the ceremonies, and that very night he went to the king to tell him what progress he had made and to receive his orders and advice about what else remained to be done.

He then visited the two queens. Madame de Clèves was not there, so she neither saw him nor, in fact, did she know of his arrival. She had heard much about this prince, as the most handsome and most charming man at the court. Madame la Dauphine had spoken of him so often, and in such glowing terms, that she was most anxious, and even quite impatient, to meet him.

She spent the entire day of the wedding preening herself for the royal ball at the Louvre. When she arrived that evening, everyone marveled at her beauty and the elegance of her attire. The ball began, and while she was dancing with Monsieur de Guise there was a great commotion near the door of the ballroom, as of someone coming in and people stepping aside. Madame de Clèves finished the dance. While she was looking around for someone for the next dance, the king called to her to dance with the gentleman who had just arrived. She turned and saw a man making his way around the seats to the dancing floor. Immediately she thought of Monsieur de Nemours. This prince was handsome in a striking sort of way: even though one had never met him before, one would notice him, especially this evening, because of the care he had taken to look his charming best, to enhance still more his distinguished manner.

It was difficult also to meet Madame de Clèves for the first time without being moved. Monsieur de Nemours was struck by her beauty. When she curtsied at his approach, he could not conceal his great admiration. They began to dance. Murmurs of praise arose in the ballroom. The king and the queen remembered that the two had never met before and thought it strange seeing them dance together without knowing each other. When they had finished their dance, before they could stop to talk to anyone, the king's party called them over to ask if each was not curious to know who the other was, or if both had guessed.

"As for me," said Monsieur de Nemours, "there is no doubt. But as Madame de Clèves has not the same reasons for knowing who I am as I have for recognizing her, I should like very much if your majesty would be good enough to tell her my name."

"I believe," said Madame la Dauphine, "that she knows it as well as you know hers."

"I assure you, Madame," replied Madame de Clèves, who seemed a little embarrassed, "that I cannot guess as well as you think I can."

"You guess very well, my dear," replied Madame la Dauphine. "There is even something very flattering in this refusal to admit to Monsieur de Nemours that, though you have never met him, you know who he is."

The queen interrupted their conversation to continue the dance, and Monsieur de Nemours danced with the queen-dauphine. This lady had seemed to Monsieur de Nemours a perfect beauty before he went to Flanders, but he now had eyes only for Madame de Clèves.

The Chevalier de Guise, who still worshipped her, was near, and what had just transpired made him more wretched. He took it as an omen that Fate itself destined Monsieur de Nemours to fall in love with Madame de Clèves. Whether indeed there was some change in her facial expression, or whether jealousy made the Chevalier de Guise put this expression there, he divined that she was visibly touched by the prince, and he could not help mentioning to her how fortunate Monsieur de Nemours was to have become acquainted with her in such an extraordinary and courtly manner.

Madame de Clèves returned home, thinking of all that had happened at the ball. Though the hour was late, she went to her mother's room to tell her all about it. She spoke to her so glowingly of Monsieur de Nemours that Madame de Chartres had the same idea as the Chevalier de Guise.

On the following day, at the Duc de Lorraine's wedding, Madame de Clèves, seeing the Duc de Nemours again, was even more impressed by his good looks and charm.

On the days that followed, she saw him with the queen-dauphine, she saw him playing tennis with the king, she saw him tilting, she heard him talk. But, in everything, she always saw him so much better than anybody else. He was in the center of every conversation—witty, charming, poised, engaging. In a short time Madame de Clèves felt she was falling in love with him.

It was also true that Monsieur de Nemours' passionate attraction to her gave him a certain air of sweetness and playfulness that often accompanies a great desire to please. Thus, he was a more interesting person than usual. Seeing each other very frequently and seeing in each other what was the best at court, it was understandable that they should be mutually charmed.

The Duchesse de Valentinois was at all the parties. For her the king still had the same lively feeling; hence he paid her the same attentions as he had when he was first in love. Madame de Clèves, who was at that age when one does not think a woman over twenty-five can be loved, was greatly surprised at the king's affection for this grandmother whose granddaughter had just been married! She often spoke of this to Madame de Chartres.

"How is it possible, Madame," she said to her, "that the king has been in love with the Duchesse de Valentinois for such a long time? How could he attach himself to a person so much older than he, who was his father's mistress, and who, from all I have heard, is still the mistress of so many?"

Replied Madame de Chartres, "It is certainly not because of Madame de Valentinois' merit or constancy that the king began to love her and still continues to do so. If she had been as young, beautiful, and virtuous as she was well-born, had she loved the king for himself and not for selfish motives, had she used her influence for his own good and the good of others, I must confess it would be difficult not to admire all this fidelity on his part.

"If I did not fear," she continued, "that you would talk about me, as people do about women of my age, saying we love to tell stories of the past, I would tell you how our king fell in love with this duchess. And I would tell you many other stories about the court of the deceased king that have much bearing on what is going on now."

"I would not talk about you, Madame," said the princess, "for telling me these stories. If I have any complaints, they would be that you have not told me enough about the various intrigues and interests at court. I am totally ignorant of them. Just a few days ago, I thought the constable and the queen were intimate friends."

"You are right," said Madame de Chartres. "Your impression was far from the truth. The queen hates M. le Connétable, and if ever she acquires any power, he will be made to feel her wrath. She knows that he has told the king many times that, of all his children, the only ones who look like him are his bastards."

"I would never have guessed this hate," interrupted Madame de Clèves, "seeing how faithfully she wrote to the M. le Connétable when he was in prison. She seemed overjoyed at his return. Why, she greets him as familiarly as she greets the king."

"If you judge by appearances at court," replied Madame de Chartres, "you will always be easily deceived, for appearances seldom lead to truth.

"But," Madame de Chartres continued, "to come back to Madame de Valentinois. You know, of course, her name is Diane de Poitiers. Her house is illustrious and she is descended from the ancient dukes of Aquitaine. One of her forebears was a bastard daughter of Louis the Eleventh. Indeed, you see, there is nothing but greatness in her family lines. Saint-Vallier, her father, was involved in an affair with the Connétable de Bourbon. He was condemned to be decapitated and was led to the scaffold. But his daughter, who was remarkably beautiful and who was already in favor with the late king, succeeded, I don't know how, in saving her father's life. They reprieved him just as he was awaiting the death blow. But he had been so terrified that he went out of his mind and died a few days later. His daughter appeared soon afterward as the king's mistress. The king's trip to Italy and his imprisonment interrupted for a short while this great love affair. When he came back from Spain, Madame the regent came to meet him in Bayonne. She brought with her all her ladies-in-waiting, among whom was a Mademoiselle de Pisseleu, who has since become the Duchesse d'Étampes. The king fell straight away in love with her. She was neither as well-born, nor as intelligent, nor as beautiful as Madame de Valentinois. The only advantage she had was her extreme youth. I have heard it said on many occasions that the Duchesse d'Étampes was born the day that Diane de Poitiers was married. But this is malicious gossip. If I am not mistaken, the Duchesse de Valentinois married Monsieur de Brézé, Sénéchal de Normandie, at the same time the king fell in love with Madame d'Étampes. Never could two women hate each other more. The Duchesse de Valentinois could not pardon Madame d'Étampes for taking from her the title of the king's mistress; Madame d'Étampes was violently jealous of Madame de Valentinois because the king still saw her. This prince was not exactly faithful to his mistresses. There was always one who enjoyed the title and honors; but the ladies, who were facetiously referred to as the "little band," each took her turn.

"The king was terribly upset by the death of his son the dauphin, who died at Tournon. The death looked suspiciously like poisoning. He did not like his second son, who is reigning now, as much as he liked the dauphin. He did not think he was sufficiently daring or vivacious. One day he complained about him to Madame de Valentinois, who said that she would make the prince fall in love with her, which would do much for his personality. She succeeded as you see. This love has lasted for more than twenty years, and neither time nor extenuating circumstances have altered his affection.

"[At first] the late king was against madame's scheme. Whether he was still so in love with Madame de Valentinois as to be jealous, or whether he was goaded by the desperate Duchesse d'Étampes—furious that Monsieur le Dauphin was in love with her enemy—it is certain that he was angered over this love affair and made no secret of it. His son feared neither his father's wrath nor his fury. Nothing could make the dauphin cool his passion nor make him hide it. The king simply adjusted to it, becoming more and more estranged from the dauphin. As a result, he gave all his attention to his third son, the Duc d'Orléans, a wild youth, fiery and ambitious, who really needed a bit of discipline. He would have made a wonderful prince if he had had enough time to mellow with age. The rivalry of the two princes existed from childhood. The high position enjoyed by the oldest, and the favor of the king enjoyed by the Duc d'Orléans, fanned this rivalry to a sort of hate. When the emperor was in France, he favored the Duc d'Orléans over the dauphin, who so bitterly resented this favoritism that when the emperor was at Chantilly, he tried to prevail upon M. le Connétable to arrest him without waiting for any orders from the king. The constable refused. Afterward, the king reprimanded him severely for not obeying the dauphin. This had a lot to do with the constable's disappearance from court.

"The animosity of the two brothers gave the Duchesse d'Étampes the idea that she could use this influence which the Duc d'Orléans had to enhance her own power over the king against Madame de Valentinois. And she was successful. Although this prince was not in love with her, he helped her in all her enterprises as much as the dauphin helped Madame de Valentinois. This made two factions at court, as you can well imagine.

"Nor were these intrigues confined only to the double

dealings of women. The emperor, who had always been on friendly terms with the Duc d'Orléans, had many times offered to him the duchy of Milan. During the peace negotiations, the emperor led him to believe that he would also hand over to him seventeen other provinces, and his daughter in marriage to boot. Monsieur le Dauphin wanted neither peace nor this marriage. He used the constable, whom he always liked, to make the king see how vitally important it was not to bequeath to his successor a brother as powerful as the Duc d'Orléans would surely be with this marriage alliance with the emperor and seventeen provinces. The constable agreed heartily with the dauphin and worked as enthusiastically in this affair as he worked against his archenemy, Madame d'Étampes, who ardently welcomed the rise of the Duc d'Orléans.

"Monsieur le Dauphin was now commanding the king's army in Champagne and had reduced the forces of the emperor to such a pitiable state that they would have been smashed, had not the Duchesse d'Étampes, fearing that too many advantages would enable us to refuse the peace, thus preventing the alliance of the emperor with the Duc d'Orléans, secretly informed the enemy that they should attack Épernay and Château-Thierry where plenty of provisions were located. They did so, and in this way saved their entire army.

"The duchesse did not for long enjoy the handiwork of her treachery. A short time afterward, Monsieur le Duc d'Orléans died at Farmoutier from some kind of contagious disease. He was in love with one of the most beautiful ladies at court and in turn was loved by her. I shall not name her because since then she has lived a very good life. She has even hidden so carefully her erstwhile love for this prince that she well deserves that we protect her reputation. By chance, she received the news of her husband's death on the same day she learned of the death of Monsieur d'Orléans, so that, you see, she was not forced to mask her sorrow.

"The king scarcely survived the prince his son; he died two years later. Before his death, he suggested to Monsieur le Dauphin that he should use as aides the Cardinal de Tournon and the Amiral d'Annebauld, never even mentioning the constable, who had been relegated to Chantilly. However, the first act of the king was to have him—the constable—recalled from exile and made head of the government. Madame d'Étampes was banished and was badly treated, as well she might have expected to be by such a powerful enemy. The Duchesse de Valentinois then had her full revenge both on Madame d'Étampes and on all those whom she did not like. Her influence over the king was more powerful than it was when he was dauphin. And so it has been for twelve years: she now is absolute mistress. She makes appointments and creates offices. She exiled the Cardinal de Tournon, Chancelier Olivier, and Villeroy. Those who have tried to enlighten the king on what was happening have been ruined.

"The Comte de Taix, grand master of the artillery, who did not care for her, could not help talking about her numerous love affairs, and especially the one with the Comte de Brissac, of whom the king was already jealous. She arranged it so well that the Comte de Taix was disgraced and relieved of his charge. But what is almost unbelievable is that this charge was given to the Comte de Brissac, and more, he was made a marshal of France. The jealousy of the king, however, reached such proportions that he could not bear to keep this marshal at court. But jealousy, which is bitter and violent in others, is mild and restrained in the king because of the affection he has for his mistress. So in this instance, he dared not exile his rival but, on some pretext, made him governor of Piedmont. Brissac stayed there many years, coming back last winter on the pretense of asking for troops and other necessary things for the army that he was commanding. But I am quite sure he returned out of longing to see Madame de Valentinois and for fear that she might forget him. The king received him coldly. The Messieurs de Guise, who don't like him, but who dare not say so because of Madame de Valentinois, used Monsieur le Vidame, who is Brissac's sworn enemy, to prevent him from obtaining anything he came to fetch. It was not difficult to thwart Brissac. The king hated him, and his presence so annoyed the king, that he was forced to go back without anything he came for, except having lighted again a flame in Madame de Valentinois' heart, which absence had begun to extinguish.

"The king has had other reasons to be jealous; but, either he is unaware of them, or he dares not complain of them.

"I don't know, my sweet," added Madame de Chartres, "if I have told you more than you wanted to know."

"No, indeed, Madame," replied Madame de Clèves. "If I did not fear inconveniencing you, I would ask you about many more things that I do not understand."

Monsieur de Nemours' passion for Madame de Clèves at first was so violent that all those women whom he had loved, and with whom he had corresponded during his absence, no longer interested him. He even forgot them. He looked for ways of saving relations; he simply could not listen to their complaints nor answer their reproaches. Madame la Dauphine, with whom he had formerly been very much in love, could not hold a candle to Madame de Clèves, and even his impatience for his trip to England waned. He was no longer making feverish preparations for departure. He paid frequent visits to the queen-dauphine because Madame de Clèves was often there; besides, it did no harm to let people think that he was still in love with this queen. Madame de Clèves seemed to him such a great catch that he resolved to fail rather in giving her signs of his affection than to hazard the chance of making this affection known to the public. He did not even talk of it to the Vidame de Chartres, his closest friend, and from whom he usually hid nothing. He behaved very sensibly, so that no one suspected his love for Madame de Clèves except the Chevalier de Guise. Madame de Clèves would scarcely have been aware of it if the inclination which she had for him had not given her an insight into her own actions which helped her understand his feelings.

At this time she did not feel inclined to discuss this prince and his infatuation with her mother as she was accustomed to do. It never occurred to her that in not speaking of him, she was not being honest. But Madame de Chartres realized it only too well. She had noticed her daughter's fondness for Monsieur de Nemours. She was greatly disturbed by the whole affair. She foresaw the terrible danger in this young girl's loving such a man as this one and being loved by him. A few days later her fears were entirely confirmed.

The Maréchal de Saint-André, who always took every opportunity to display his great wealth, asked the king, on the pretext of showing him his new house, to do him the honor of dining with him. the invitation included the two queens. This marshal was equally eager that Madame de Clèves also should see what enormous sums of money he had spent.

Some days before this supper the king-dauphin, whose health was none too stable, became sick and could see no one. The queen his wife spent the whole day at his bedside. Toward evening, feeling much better, he sent for all the people in the antechamber. The queen-dauphine went back to her own apartment. She found there Madame de Clèves and a few other close friends.

Since it was already late, and she was not dressed, she did not go to the queen's, but gave orders that she wanted to see no one that evening. She sent for her jewels to select some to wear at the Maréchal de Saint-André's dinner and others which she had promised to lend to Madame de Clèves.

While they were busy doing this, the Prince de Condé arrived. The queen-dauphine said that no doubt he was coming from the king her husband, and she asked him what they were doing there.

"They are arguing with Monsieur de Nemours," he replied. "He is defending his point so vehemently that you might think it was something of personal concern. I think he has some mistress who is causing him anxiety because she is coming to a ball. He says it is annoying to see a person whom you love at a dance."

"What's this!" said Madame la Dauphine. "Monsieur de Nemours doesn't want his mistress to go to a ball? I knew that husbands did not wish their wives to go, but, as for lovers, I never thought that they had any such notions."

"Well, Monsieur de Nemours is of the opinion," replied the Prince de Condé, "that there is nothing more unbearable than dances for lovers, who are loved or not loved in return. He says that even if they are loved, for several days they must be resigned to less of her attention, because there is no woman in the world who does not give more care to her attire than to her lover. With this business she is entirely preoccupied. Furthermore, this primping is done more to impress the world than the one she loves. And when she is at the dance, she wishes to please those who are gaping at her. The satisfaction she derives from looking beautiful bears no relationship to her lover. It is his opinion, too, that when you are not loved, you suffer still more seeing your mistress at public functions. The more she's admired, the more miserable you are not to be loved by her. You are always fearful that her beauty will start an affair more fortunate than your own. In short, he thinks that there is no suffering quite comparable to that of seeing the one you love at a ball, unless it be knowing she is there and you are not."

Madame de Clèves pretended not to hear what the Prince de Condé was saying, but she had listened with much attention. She judged easily what part she had played in the formulation of Monsieur de Nemours' ideas, and she felt especially responsible for what he had to say about the wretchedness of a lover not being at a ball his mistress was attending. It so happened Monsieur de Nemours would not be at this supper of the Maréchal de Saint-André, since the king was sending him on a mission to the Duke of Ferrara.

The queen-dauphine and the Prince de Condé were laughing because they did not at all hold Monsieur de Nemours' opinions.

"There is only one instance, Madame," said Monsieur de Condé, "when Monsieur de Nemours would consent to the mistress attending a public ball—that is when the lover was giving it. He said that last year, when he gave one for your highness, his mistress favored him by coming, although she came only on your account. He says that it is showing respect to a lover to go to one of his affairs and that it flatters him when he can show his mistress how well and properly he entertains the entire court."

"Monsieur de Nemours was right," said the queen-dauphine, with a smile, "in approving his mistresses' attendance at his ball, because having so many ladies at that time who were his mistresses, had they not come, few would have been there indeed."

As soon as the Prince de Condé had begun to talk about Monsieur de Nemours' views on dances, Madame de Clèves decided then and there not to go to Saint-André's ball. She could easily agree that you should not go to the house of the man who overly admires you, and she was delighted to have found a good reason for doing something that would please with Monsieur de Nemours. However, she did accept the jewels which the queen-dauphine was lending her. But that evening, when she showed them to her mother, she casually remarked that she had no intention of using them. By way of explanation, she complained that the Maréchal de Saint-André was always paying her too many annoying attentions, which broadcast to all his obvious affection. Also, she did not doubt that he wished her to believe that she would have a part in the entertainment of the king, and that that situation, in turn, would serve as an indication of the affection in which she was held by the marshal. This indication of emotion she would find embarrassing.

Madame de Chartres disputed for a while these ideas of her daughter, finding them a little picayune. But seeing that her mind was made up, Madame de Chartres gave in and told her she must pretend illness in order to have a suitable pretext for not attending, because the reasons proffered certainly would not be approved and everyone would look upon them suspiciously. Madame de Clèves gladly agreed to stay home for a few days so that she would not have to go to a dance where Monsieur de Nemours would not be in attendance. He left Paris without the pleasure of knowing she was staying at home.

When he came back, the day after the ball, he learned that she had not gone. Since he did not know that someone had repeated to her his conversation at the dauphin's, it never occurred to him that it was on account of him that she did not go to the dance.

Next day, at the queen's, while he was talking to Madame la Dauphine, Madame de Chartres and Madame de Clèves arrived. Madame de Clèves was not dressed in her usual style, appearing like a person who had been sick. But her face did not match her dress.

"You look so beautiful," said Madame la Dauphine, "that I cannot believe you have been ill. I think that Monsieur the Prince de Condé, when telling us of Monsieur de Nemours' ideas on dances, convinced you that by going to the marshal's dinner and ball, you would be honoring the Maréchal de Saint-André. Perhaps that is why you didn't go."

Madame de Clèves blushed at Madame la Dauphine's accurate guess made in Monsieur de Nemours' presence. Madame de Chartres realized immediately why her daughter had not wanted to go to the ball, and to prevent Monsieur de Nemours from guessing it too, she spoke with an air of forced sincerity.

"I assure you, Madame, that your majesty is giving my daughter more credit than she deserves. She was really ill, and I believe, had I not stopped her, she would have gone anyway, just for the pleasure of seeing all the delightful entertainment at the celebration last night."

Madame la Dauphine believed Madame de Chartres. Monsieur de Nemours was grieved, though the explanation seemed plausible enough. However, Madame de Clèves' blushes made him suspect that what Madame la Dauphine had said might not be too far from the truth. Madame de Clèves, at first upset because Monsieur de Nemours thought he himself was the cause of her absence from the ball, felt something akin to annoyance that her mother had so entirely dispelled this idea of his.

Although the conference at Cercamp had broken up, peace negotiations still continued and, indeed, made such real progress that the conference reconvened with the same delegates at Cateau-Cambrésis. The absence of the Maréchal de Saint-André deprived Monsieur de Nemours of a rival who was formidable more on account of Saint-André's interest in the maneuverings of other suitors of Madame de Clèves than by any progress the marshal could himself make with her.

Madame de Chartres did not want her daughter to know that she was aware of the girl's feelings for Monsieur de Nemours, for fear of making her anticipate a subject her mother wished to broach at a later date.

One day Madame de Chartres did begin talking about Monsieur de Nemours, observing, however, after she praised his better qualities, that he was incapable of falling in love, that he sought after the company of women for pleasure's sake and not for any serious reason. "Everybody," she added, "and rightly so, suspects that he is madly in love with the queen-dauphine. Certainly, he visits her frequently enough. I would advise you to avoid, as much as you are able, talking to him, particularly when alone, on account of your relationship with Madame la Dauphine. People might say you were their

confidante, and you know how unpleasant that reputation is! It is my opinion, if this rumor continues, you
would do well to see less of Madame la Dauphine so as
not to get yourself too involved in this love affair."

Madame de Clèves had never heard Monsieur de
Nemours linked with Madame la Dauphine. She was so
surprised by what her mother said, and so convinced now
that she had been mistaken about the real feelings of this
prince for herself, that the expression on her face changed
perceptibly, and Madame de Chartres noticed it. At this
moment, some people arrived; so Madame de Clèves
went home and shut herself up in her room.

Words cannot describe how her heart ached; her mother
had just made her realize what she had not dared to
admit to herself—she was falling in love with Monsieur
de Nemours. She was quick to see that her feelings for
him were exactly those which Monsieur de Clèves had so
much craved. She was ashamed to have these feelings for
one not her husband, who rightfully deserved them. She
felt hurt and embarrassed because Monsieur de Nemours
had only wanted to make use of her in his affair with
Madame la Dauphine. This thought made her decide to
tell Madame de Chartres what she had up to this point
hidden from her.

So, the next morning, resolutely, she went to her mother's room, but finding her mother with a slight fever, she
postponed talking to her.

That evening after dinner, because Madame de Chartres
did not seem to be too seriously ill, Madame de Clèves
betook herself to Madame la Dauphine, who was at
home with two or three of her closest friends.

When Madame de Clèves entered, the dauphine said,
"We were just talking about Monsieur de Nemours and
were remarking how he has changed since his return
from Brussels. Before he went there, he had a score of
mistresses. In fact, this was a fault with him. And he
treated them all alike, whether they were meritorious of
his affections or not. But now since his return, he doesn't

recognize any of them. I have never seen in a man such a change. Why, I do believe even his disposition has changed—he isn't as carefree as he used to be."

Madame de Clèves did not say a word. Rather shamefully, she thought that, had she not been disillusioned, she would have taken all that was said of Monsieur de Nemours' change for marks of his love for herself. She felt some rancor toward Madame la Dauphine for pretending to probe for reasons and to be surprised at something about which she knew the truth probably better than anyone. She could not resist letting Madame la Dauphine know a little of what she was thinking. So, when the other ladies left, she went up and said to her almost in a whisper: "Were these words, Madame, for me? Would you hide from me that it is on your account that Monsieur de Nemours has changed so?"

"You are unfair," replied the dauphine. "You know that I have nothing to hide from you. It is true that Monsieur de Nemours, before going to Brussels, did intend, I believe, to let me understand that he didn't exactly hate me. But, since his return, it doesn't seem to me he even remembers what went on before. I confess I am very curious to find out what has made him such a changed person. It will be difficult, but I shall get to the bottom of it." She added, "The Vidame de Chartres, who is an intimate friend of his, is in love with a person over whom I have some influence, and I shall find out through her what has brought about this change."

Madame la Dauphine spoke convincingly, and Madame de Clèves, in spite of herself, felt more assured and better relaxed than before.

When she returned home, she learned that her mother's condition had become much worse. The fever was higher. On the following days her temperature rose still more, so that quite obviously she was very sick indeed. Madame de Clèves, terribly distraught, did not leave her mother's room. Monsieur de Clèves went there almost every day too, genuinely concerned about Madame de

Chartres' condition, and anxious to comfort his wife, but more importantly for the pleasure of seeing his wife, whom he loved very much.

Monsieur de Nemours, who had always been friendly with Monsieur de Clèves, had not ceased being so since his return from Brussels. During the illness of Madame de Chartres, he had many occasions to see Madame de Clèves. Sometimes he would make his appearance on the pretext that he came to call for her husband to walk in the country. Sometimes he would call, knowing full well that he would not be there, but pretending to wait for him in Madame de Chartres' antechamber, where there were always several of her close friends. Madame de Clèves was frequently there, and, for all her grief, to Monsieur de Nemours she was no less beautiful. He took great pains to let her see how he sympathized with her in this moment of trial, and he spoke so kindly and sweetly to her of her trouble that she was convinced it was not Madame la Dauphine whom he loved. In his presence she could not help but feel a certain pleasant anguish. When he was not there, the thought that his presence could ignite her affection almost made her believe she hated him.

Madame de Chartres became considerably worse. Everybody, including the doctors, began to despair of her life. She received the news of her imminent danger with a courage worthy of her goodness and piety. After the doctors had left, she made everyone leave and called for Madame de Clèves.

"I am going to leave you," she said to Madame de Clèves, taking her daughter's hand, "and the danger in which I leave you, and the need you have of me now, only make me more sorrowful. You are attracted to Monsieur de Nemours; I don't ask you to confess it. I am no longer in any condition to guide you. I have known of your affection for a long time, but did not wish to say anything at first for fear that you might not be aware of it yourself. Now you know it only too well. My dear, you are on the brink of a precipice. To keep yourself from going over, great moral constraint is required. Think of what you owe to your husband; think, my sweet of what you owe to yourself. Reflect on the reputation you stand to lose—a reputation patiently formed and so much desired by me. Have strength and courage, my dear. Leave the court. Compel your husband to take you away. However rude, difficult, frightening these drastic measures may seem to be at first, they will be more pleasant in the end than the wretchedness of a sordid affair. If I cannot prevail upon you to do as I wish for reasons other than virtue or duty, let me confess that if anything could destroy the happiness I hope for in leaving this world, it would be to see you fall to the level of other women. If this should be your misfortune, I would joyfully welcome death to avoid being a witness to this calamity."

Madame de Clèves burst into tears. She held her mother's hand tightly in her own, and Madame de Chartres was deeply moved. "Adieu, my child," she said to her, "let us finish with this sad conversation which is upsetting us so. But remember, if you will, all that I have told you."

Having finished, and not wanting to listen or to say any more, she turned away, ordering her daughter to bid the ladies come in.

You can imagine in what state Madame de Clèves left her mother's room; she thought of nothing else but her mother's end. Madame de Chartres lived another two days, during which time she had no desire to see again the only thing she ever really loved—her daughter.

Madame de Clèves was in a terrible state. Her husband never left her side, and as soon as Madame de Chartres died, he took his wife to the country to be far from surroundings which could only increase the bitterness of her sorrow. No grief was like hers. The love she bore her mother, the gratitude she owed her, the protection she needed against Monsieur de Nemours only intensified her anguish. Unhappy and abandoned at a time when she was so little in control of her emotions, she now longed for someone who could sympathize with her and give the much needed strength. The manner in which Monsieur de Clèves had been of help made her more resolute not to be wanting in anything she owed him. She was friendlier and sweeter to him than she had ever been. She never wanted to leave him, for it seemed to her that her defense against Monsieur de Nemours depended upon how well she forged the bonds of attachment to her husband.

Monsieur de Nemours came often to visit Monsieur de Clèves in the country, and did what he could at the same time to see madame, but she would not receive him. She resolved not to see him at any cost, knowing too well how his presence would affect her.

Monsieur de Clèves went to Paris on an errand. He promised his wife he would return on the morrow. But he came back instead two days later.

"I waited for you yesterday," Madame de Clèves said to him when he arrived, "and I could reproach you for not returning when you promised. You must know that, if I could feel any more grief in my present state, it would be that caused by the death of Madame de Tournon, of which I learned this morning. Even had I not known her, I would have been sorry, for it is always sad when a woman young and pretty as she was dies in two days. But, more than that, she was one whom I liked, because she always struck me as wise and good."

"I am sorry for not returning yesterday," said Monsieur de Clèves, "but I really had to stay in Paris to console a poor unfortunate friend of mine. As for Madame de Tournon, if you are mourning her death because she was a wise and proper person, I would caution you not to be too upset by it."

"You surprise me," replied Madame de Clèves. "Why, I have heard you say many times that there was no woman at court whom you admired more!"

"That's true. I did say that, but, my dear, women are

such incomprehensible creatures, and when I am in their company, I realize how happy, and, indeed, fortunate I am in having you!"

"You esteem me more than I am worth," sighed Madame de Clèves. "I am not yet worthy of your high regard. Tell me, please, I beg you, what has caused your disillusionment with her."

"For a long time now, I have known of her deceitful ways. I knew she loved the Comte de Sancerre. She had promised even to marry him."

"I cannot believe it!" interrupted Madame de Clèves. "Why everyone knows that she has publicly declared she would never remarry. How could she possibly have made such promises to Sancerre?"

"If he were the only one she had promised," said Monsieur de Clèves, "it would not have been so frightfully bad—but, at the very same time, she was also making promises to Estouteville. Let me tell you the whole story."

BOOK 2

❧

"You know how friendly we were, Sancerre and I; nevertheless, about two years ago he fell in love with Madame de Tournon, and took great pains to hide the fact from me as well as from everybody else. I never suspected it, because Madame de Tournon still seemed distraught and inconsolable over the recent death of her husband. She hardly saw anyone or went anywhere, except to visit with Sancerre's sister, and it was there that he fell in love with her.

"One evening, when there was to be a play at the Louvre, and when we were all there waiting for the king and Madame de Valentinois to arrive so that it might begin, word was brought that Madame de Valentinois was ill and for this reason the king would not be coming. Everybody concluded that this "illness" of the duchess was really some quarrel with the king. We all knew how jealous he was of the Maréchal de Brissac when this gentleman was at court. But he had returned to Piedmont a few days previously, and we just could not imagine why they might be quarreling.

"While I was speaking about it to Sancerre, Monsieur d'Anville came into the room, approached me, and confidentially informed me that the king was upset and in a pitiable state of anger, that a few days ago, in a reconciliation between him and Madame de Valentinois, over the unpleasant dealings with the Maréchal de Brissac, the king had given her a ring and had requested that she wear it. While she was dressing to come to the theater, the king noticed that she was not wearing this ring and he asked her why. She appeared to be surprised not to have it and asked her attendants, who, unhappily, or for want of being properly forewarned, replied that they had not seen it for four or five days. Now this time," continued Monsieur d'Anville, "coincided precisely with the Marshal de Brissac's departure. The king has no doubt at all that she gave him the ring when they said good-by to each other. This so aroused his jealous heart that he flew into a rage, which is not like him at all, and he reproached her severely. D'Anville said that the king had just gone back to his apartment very angry. But D'Anville didn't know whether the king is angered because Madame de Valentinois gave away his ring or upset for fear he might have displeased her with his fit of temper.

"As soon as Monsieur d'Anville finished telling me this bit of news, I went over to Sancerre and told him, begging him to keep all this confidential since someone had just confided it to me as a secret.

"The next morning, rather early, I went to my sister-in-law's. Madame de Tournon was there by her bed. She had no love for Madame de Valentinois, and she knew my sister-in-law had no particular affection for her either. Sancerre, after the play, had gone to Madame de Tournon's and told her of the quarrel between the king and the duchess. Madame de Tournon had come to tell the story to my sister-in-law, without knowing or suspecting that it was I who had given the story to her lover.

"As soon as I arrived, my sister-in-law said to Madame de Tournon that I could be trusted with this secret, and without waiting for Madame de Tournon's permission, she recited word for word everything I had confided to Sancerre the night before. You can imagine my surprise. I looked at Madame de Tournon; she seemed embarrassed, and this made me suspicious. I had told the story only to Sancerre. He had left me abruptly at the end of the play, without giving any explanation, and I remembered hearing him speak of Madame de Tournon in glowing terms. All these things opened my eyes. It didn't take me long to figure out that it was with her he was having an affair and that it was she whom he visited when he left me. I was so incensed because he had hidden this affair from me that I said many things to let Madame de Tournon know how imprudent she had been. I led her to her carriage, and assured her, when taking my leave, that I envied the good fortune of the gentleman who had told her of the spat between the king and Madame de Valentinois.

"I went immediately to find Sancerre to reproach his indiscretion and to tell him I knew of his love for Madame de Tournon. I didn't tell him, however, how I learned of it. He was forced to admit it. It was then I told him how I found out, and he narrated all the details of their affair, telling me that, although he was the youngest in his family, and very far from being a good match for her, she was, nevertheless, determined to marry him. No one could have been more surprised than I was. I told Sancerre that he had better hurry up and marry her, since there was nothing he might not expect of a woman so clever in deceiving the public. He replied that she had indeed been distressed over her husband's death, but that her love for him had helped her to overcome her grief, but that she did not yet want a sudden change in appearances. He told me of other reasons he had for excusing her, which made me keenly aware to what extent he was in love with this woman. He assured me that he would reconcile her to the idea of his telling me of their love affair since it was she anyway who had first made me suspect it. With a lot of difficulty, he did secure her agreement to this idea, and from that time on I was very much in their confidence.

"I have never seen a woman so openly honest, so charming with her lover. Yet I was shocked to see how affectedly sad she appeared before the public. Sancerre was so much in love and so satisfied with her behavior toward him that he dared not rush her into their marriage, for fear she might think he was marrying her more for material gains than for love. Nevertheless, he did speak to her about their marriage, and she still seemed quite determined to go through with their plans.

"Soon she began coming out of hiding and taking part in social gatherings, sometimes going to my sister-in-law's at that time of day when some of the court would be present. Sancerre went only on rare occasions, but those who did attend these gatherings every evening, and who saw Madame de Tournon there, thought her charming.

"A little later, after she had begun to go out more often, Sancerre thought he detected some coolness in her affections for him. He spoke to me about it many times, but I didn't give his complaints any serious attention. However, when he told me that instead of getting closer to a marriage date, she seemed to be postponing it, I began to believe he had some basis for his anxiety. I answered him that it would not be surprising in the least if Madame de Tournon's passion, having lasted two years, should begin to lessen, that even if it had not lessened, he ought not to complain if it were not strong enough to constrain her to marry him. I told him that in the eyes of the court, this marriage would do him no good, since it wasn't a good match for her and certainly would compromise her reputation. I indicated that all he could rightfully expect was that she be honest with him, that she offer him no false hopes. Furthermore, I stated even if she felt she could not marry him and even told him that she loved another, he ought not to be angry, nor would he have any reason to complain. Still he owed her respect and gratitude.

"I am giving you, I told him, the same advice I would give myself. Believe me, I value sincerity above everything else. If my mistress, or even my wife, should sincerely and frankly confess that she loved another, I would be pained but not embittered. I would stop being her

lover, or her husband, as the case might be, in order to
help her and to sympathize with her."

At these words Madame de Clèves blushed. What he
was saying was relevant and was surprisingly applicable
to her own situation. She was disturbed and was a long
time regaining her composure.

"Sancerre spoke to Madame de Tournon," continued
Monsieur de Clèves. "He told her of the counsel I had
given to him, but she reassured him, and, indeed, she
seemed so offended by this suspicion that she went to
great pains to remove it completely from his mind. Nevertheless, she put off the marriage until after a rather
long trip that he was going to take. Right up to the day of
departure, she treated him so well and seemed so distressed by his leaving that I did believe, like Sancerre,
that she really loved him. He left about two months ago.
During his absence I saw little of Madame de Tournon. I
knew Sancerre was returning shortly.

"The day before yesterday, arriving in Paris, I learned
of her death. I sent to his house to inquire if there was
any news from him. They told me he had returned the
day before, on the very day of her death.

"I immediately hurried to him, thinking of the state in
which I would probably find him, but his sorrow sur-
passed my worst fears. I have never seen a man so
distressed. As soon as he saw me, he embraced me and
broke down and wept.

" 'I shall not see her any more,' he sobbed. 'I shall not
see her any more! She is dead, dead, dead! Do you hear
me. I was not worthy of her. But follow her, I will!'

"After that, he became silent. And then, intermit-
tently, he would repeat: 'She is dead; I shall see her no
more!' He began crying again; tears filled his eyes, and
he looked like a man who has lost his reason.

"He told me that during his absence he had received
very few letters from her, but he was not surprised at
this, since he knew sending letters would be a bit of a
nuisance to her. He did not doubt for a minute that she

would marry him upon his return; he looked up to her as the most lovable, the most faithful person in the world. He thought himself just as tenderly loved by her. Now he had lost her just when it seemed he possessed her forever. All these painful thoughts plunged him into a veritable dark sea of sorrow. I was moved to deep pity.

"But I was obliged to leave him to go to the king. I promised him that I would return shortly.

"I did, in fact, come back later, and I was never so surprised as I was to find him so completely changed in mood from a little earlier. He was standing in his room, furiously angered, walking up and down, as if totally beside himself with rage.

" 'Come in! Come!' he said. 'Behold the most miserable man in the world. I am a thousand times more wretched than I was a little while ago because what I have just learned about Madame de Tournon is far worse than news of her death.'

"At first I thought he was just overcome with emotion. I could not imagine what could possibly be worse than the death of a loved one by whom he was loved in return. I told him that as long as his sorrow had been kept within bounds, I understood and sympathized with him; but I could no longer feel sorry for a person who abandoned himself to such despair and such irrational antics as these.

" 'I would only be too happy to have lost my reason, even to be dead,' he screamed. 'Madame de Tournon was unfaithful to me! And to think I have learned of her treachery only the day after I learned of her death—at a time when my soul was filled with the tenderest emotions of love and pierced with the sharpest arrows of grief; at a time when a most perfect image of her—perfect toward me—was seared eternally in my heart, I find that I have been deceived and that she is unworthy of my tears. But, curiously, I feel as much sorrow over her death as I would if she had been faithful, and as much grief over her infidelity as I would if she were not dead. Had I only discovered her infidelity before her death, jealousy, anger and rage would have consumed me and hardened me in some way to the grief caused by her loss! But now in this wretched state I can neither console myself nor hate her.'

"You can readily imagine how surprised I was by what Sancerre told me. I asked him how he came upon this information. He told me that right after I had left his room, Estouteville, who was his closest friend but who knew nothing of his love for Madame de Tournon, had come to see him. He said that as soon as he was seated Estouteville began to weep, sobbing that Sancerre must pardon him for having hidden what he was about to tell him, saying that Sancerre must pity him instead, that he was coming to open his heart, that because of Madame de Tournon's death he was the world's most wretched creature.

" 'This name,' Sancerre said, 'so surprised me, that although my first inclination was to confess that I was more afflicted by her death than he, I was speechless. Estouteville continued, saying that he had been in love with her for six months, that he had always intended to tell me of this love but that she had expressly forbidden him to do so, and with such firmness, that he dared not disobey her. He said that they had fallen in love almost at first sight, keeping their love a secret from everyone; that never once was he seen publicly in her house; that he had consoled her for the death of her husband. He told me that he was about to marry her when she died; but that this marriage, which indeed would be one of love, was to appear a result of duty and obedience since she had convinced her father to make him order her to marry Estouteville so that her attitude toward remarriage would not appear so drastically changed.

" 'While Estouteville was speaking,' said Sancerre to me, 'I believed him; it all seemed to be true, because at the time when he said he had fallen in love with Madame de Tournon—that is precisely the time when I had noticed a change in her. A moment later I thought him a liar or, at the very least, a victim of his own hallucinations, and I was ready to tell him so. I wanted to clarify some details, so I questioned him, making it appear that I doubted his story. Finally, I had many details to assure me of my unhappiness. Then he asked me if I knew Madame de Tournon's handwriting. He laid on my bed four of her letters and her portrait.

" 'At that moment my brother entered. Estouteville's face was so drenched with tears that he was forced to leave for fear of being seen. He said that he would return later in the evening to get these things he was leaving with me. Then I got rid of my brother on the pretext that I was ill. I was burning with impatience to read these letters, which Estouteville had left with me. I was hoping that there would be something in them to convince me that what Estouteville had said was all a lie! But alas! What did I find? What tenderness! What promises! What assurances that she would marry him! What passionate letters! Never had she written such letters to me! So,' he added, 'I am suffering on two accounts: her death, and her treachery—two misfortunes often compared to each other but never simultaneously experienced by the same person. I swear, shamefully, that I still feel more her death than I do her infidelities. I cannot find it in me to be happy over her death. If she were alive, I would have the pleasure of reproaching her, of having my revenge by making her realize the injustice of it all.'

" 'But I shall see her no more,' he began again, 'I shall see her no more. And this will be the greatest of all my ills. Oh, that I could bring her back to life in exchange for my own! But what a wish is this! Were she alive, she would live only for Estouteville!

" 'In truth how happy I was yesterday,' he cried, 'how very happy! I was the sorriest man in the world, but at least my sorrow was reasonable and I found some sweetness in thinking that I could not and would not be consoled. Today all my thoughts are awry. I am paying dearly for the pretended passion she had for me—the same tribute of sorrow that I thought owing a true love. I can neither hate nor love the memory of her; I can neither be consoled nor grieved over her death.'

" 'At least,' he said suddenly turning toward me, 'I beseech you, never let me see Estouteville again—I hate the very sound of his name. I know I have no reason to; it is my fault for hiding from him that I loved Madame de Tournon. If he had known of it, perhaps he would not have fallen in love with her, and perhaps, too, she would not have been unfaithful to me. He came looking for me to confide his sorrow. He made me pity him. Eh! And with reason,' he cried. 'He loved Madame de Tournon, she loved him. Now he will never see her again. But I still hate him. I can't help myself. And once again, I beg you, arrange it so that I never see him please.' "

Monsieur de Clèves continued, "Sancerre began to weep again and to mourn for Madame de Tournon, to speak to her, and to tell her sweet tender thoughts. His mood then changed to hate, to complaints, to reproaches, to imprecations against her. When I saw him thus, in such a dreadful state, I knew that I would need help to calm him, so I sent for his brother whom I had just left at the king's apartment. When he arrived, I spoke to him in the antechamber about Sancerre's desperate emotional state. We gave orders to prevent him from seeing Estouteville, and we spent the greater part of the night trying to bring Sancerre to his senses. This morning I found him still upset; his brother remained by his side and I came back to you."

"This is terrible!" said Madame de Clèves, "and I thought she was incapable both of love and of deceit."

"No one person could have been craftier, more deceitful than she," replied Monsieur de Clèves. "Notice that when Sancerre thought she was behaving differently toward him, she was indeed, because at this time she was falling in love with Estouteville. She told Estouteville he was her consolation after the death of her husband and was the cause of her leaving her retreatlike existence, while all the time Sancerre thought she was so acting on his account. She wanted Estouteville to keep their love affair secret so that she could make it appear it was her father who was forcing her to marry him, pretending that it was for the sake of his reputation; but she acted in this fashion to sever more easily relations with Sancerre, who would have then really no reason to complain.

"I must go back," continued Monsieur de Clèves, "to see this poor chap, and I think you should return to Paris, also. It is time you saw some people and did some entertaining."

Madame agreed to return, and she went back the following day.

She was much calmer about Monsieur de Nemours than before. Everything Madame de Chartres had said to her on her deathbed, and the sadness over her mother's death, checked her feeling for him so that she believed their attachment was quite finished.

The very evening she arrived in Paris, Madame la Dauphine came to see her. After expressing her condolences, in order to distract her from these sad thoughts, the dauphine began to inform Madame de Clèves about everything that had happened at court during her absence.

She divulged some choice bits of news: "But what I am dying to tell you," she said, "is that Monsieur de Nemours is passionately in love for sure, and that his closest friends not only don't know, but they can't even guess who the lady might be! Moreover, this love, my dear, is strong enough to make him neglect—I should rather say abandon —any hopes for a crown."

Madame la Dauphine then told about everything that had been happening over his English project. "I learned it from Monsieur d'Anville," she confided. "He told me this morning that yesterday evening the king sent for Monsieur de Nemours to inform him about certain letters received from Lignerolles. It seems that Lignerolles wrote to the king requesting to be recalled because he can no longer make excuses to the Queen of England for Monsieur de Nemours' delay; she is beginning to be offended by it in fact, because, even though she had not committed herself positively, she did say enough for him to risk the journey. The king read this letter to Monsieur de Nemours, who instead of speaking seriously as he had in the beginning, only laughed and joked and made slight of Lignerolles' whimsical hopes. He said all Europe would reproach him for imprudence if he chanced a trip to England as a prospective match for the queen without any guarantees of its success. 'It seems to me,' Monsieur de Nemours went on, 'that it would be an ill-chosen time to go to England anyway, since presently the King of Spain is making such a concerted effort to marry this queen. Perhaps in a love affair he would not be a serious rival, but I think, when it comes to marriage, your majesty would not advise that I oppose the King of Spain.'

" 'In this case, I would advise it,' replied the king. 'He wouldn't be a rival; I happen to know he has other ideas. But even if he had not, Queen Mary found the yoke of Spain fraught with too many problems for anyone to believe that her sister would wish it back again or that she would be dazzled by the prospects of joining together so many kingdoms.'

" 'If she be not dazzled,' Monsieur de Nemours countered, 'it does seem she would like to be made happy by love. Some years back she was in love with Lord Courtenay; Queen Mary loved him too and would have married him, with the blessings of all England, had she not realized that the youth and beauty of her sister Elizabeth touched him more than the hope of reigning. Your majesty knows full well that her violent jealousies constrained her to put them both into prison, then to exile Lord Courtenay, and to marry out of spite the King of Spain. I think that Elizabeth, who is now on the throne, will soon go back to this Lord Courtenay and that she will choose this man whom she has already loved, who is very handsome, and who has suffered so much for her, rather than choose another whom she has never seen.'

" 'I would be inclined to agree with you,' said the king, 'if Lord Courtenay were still alive, but I have known for several days that he died in Padua where he was exiled. I see,' he added taking his leave of Monsieur de Nemours, 'that we will have to arrange your marriage as we did with Monsieur le Dauphin, that is, arrange this wedding with the Queen of England through ambassadors.' "

The dauphine continued, "Monsieur d'Anville and Monsieur le Vidame, who were present, are convinced that it is this new passion of his which has made him decide against this scheme to marry the Queen of England. The vidame, who sees him more often than anyone, told Madame de Martiques that De Nemours has changed so that it is hard to recognize him. And what is most curious is that he doesn't seem to have any engagements with anyone, nor any special hours when he must steal away. In fact, D'Anville thinks there is no understanding with this person whom he loves, that seeing Monsieur de Nemours love a woman who does not return it is most unusual."

For Madame de Clèves this long chat with Madame la Dauphine was poison! How could she fail to recognize this person whose name no one knew? How could she not help feeling grateful and tender, learning that this prince, who already stirred her heart, was hiding his love for her from everyone and was abandoning, for her sake, his prospects for a throne? One cannot possibly describe her feelings at this moment. New storms brewed in her soul.

If Madame la Dauphine had watched her closely, she would have easily realized that Madame de Clèves was not at all indifferent to the story just related. But, since she had no suspicion of its relevancy, she went on speaking, giving no heed to her words:

"Monsieur d'Anville," she added, "who, as I have just told you, informed me of all these details, thinks I know more than he does. He thinks me so charming that he is sure I am the only person who could possibly effect such drastic changes in Monsieur de Nemours."

These last words of Madame la Dauphine stirred Madame de Clèves, but she said, "I share Monsieur d'Anville's opinion. It is very likely, Madame, that it would have to be a princess—someone like yourself—to make Monsieur de Nemours become suddenly uninterested in the Queen of England."

"I would tell you if I knew," Madame la Dauphine replied, "and if it were true, I would know it. Such passions do not easily escape the notice of those who are responsible for them. Indeed they are the first to take notice. Monsieur de Nemours has never shown me but slight attention, Madame. There is such a difference in the way he has behaved toward me in the past from the way he approaches me now, that I can assure you positively it is not I who caused him to pass up the throne of England.

"I am forgetful when I am with you," added Madame la Dauphine, "so I don't recall if I am to go to see Madame. You know that the peace treaty is almost concluded, but you do not know that the King of Spain did not wish to pass on any of its articles, excepting on condition that this princess should marry him, instead of his son Don Carlos. The king had much difficulty making up his mind, but in the end he did consent, and now he has gone to announce this news to Madame. I think she will be inconsolable. It is no easy task to marry a man with the age and temperament of the King of Spain; especially for one so young, so gay, so beautiful, who was hopeful of marrying a prince for whom she felt some attraction even though she has never seen him. I really don't know if the king will find in her all the submissiveness he so desires. He asked me to go see her because he knows she likes me and he thinks I might have some influence over her.

"Afterward, however, I shall make another very different kind of visit: I shall go to rejoice with Madame the king's sister. Everything has come to a stop in preparation for her marriage with the Duc de Savoie, who will be here shortly. Never has a princess of her age been so delighted to marry. This court is going to be more brilliant and more crowded than you have ever seen it. In spite of your mourning, you must come to show these foreigners that we have beautiful women at court, too."

When she finished, Madame la Dauphine left Madame de Clèves. The following day the whole world knew of the plans for Madame's marriage.

On days that followed, the king and the two queens came to visit with Madame de Clèves. Monsieur de Nemours, who had awaited her return with extreme impatience and who wanted so much to be alone with her, waited to call on her at an hour when everyone had gone and it seemed unlikely anyone would return. His plan worked. He arrived just as the last visitors were leaving.

Madame de Clèves was on her bed; it was hot. The sight of Monsieur de Nemours made her blush, which in no way detracted from her beauty. He sat down facing her with a sort of fear and nervousness that are marks of deep emotion. For a few minutes there was silence. Madame de Clèves was not less disconcerted.

Finally it was Monsieur de Nemours who spoke. He expressed his condolences on her recent loss. Madame de Clèves, who was very pleased to pursue this particular line of conversation, spoke for a rather long time on the death of her mother, saying, though time would mitigate the violence of her sorrow, nevertheless, such an indelible impression of it had been made that she thought her outlook would be quite changed.

"Great sorrow and violent passions," he observed, "do bring about great changes in our thinking. Even I, since my return from Flanders, don't recognize myself. Many people have remarked this change in me, and even Madame la Dauphine spoke of it again yesterday."

"That's correct," said Madame de Clèves, "she is aware

of it, and I do seem to recall her having made some mention of it."

"I am not sorry she notices it," said Monsieur de Nemours, "but I would she were not the only one to have observed it. There could be a certain situation in which one dare not declare his love openly; but, even so, he would wish that this person at least would see that he is not loved by any other; that she would realize that there is no other beauty, whatever her rank, who could impress him; that there is no throne one would wish to purchase at the price of never seeing her again. A woman ordinarily measures a man's love," he went on, "by the trouble he takes to please her and to seek her company. But this is no trouble if she has even a modicum of charm. What is difficult is to resist the pleasure of her company and to avoid her lest these sentiments become obvious to her and to the public. The mark of true affection is rather gauged by the complete change it effects in the life of the lover, how it has altered the course of his life's ambitions and accustomed pleasures."

Madame de Clèves readily understood that his words were directed to her. She felt that she ought to answer him, that she ought not allow him to go on. She felt that she ought not to listen, that she ought not by any display show that his words were meant for her. She thought it was her duty both to speak and to say nothing. What he said pleased and offended her. She saw in his words a confirmation of all the thoughts Madame la Dauphine had engendered. She found them gallant and respectful, but also somewhat daring and all too revealing. The attraction she had for this prince caused sensations over which she had no control. She realized that the most shaded remarks from a man of whom one is very fond can cause more agitation in one's heart than the most open declarations from a man for whom one feels no attraction at all. So she did not answer, and Monsieur de Nemours would have noticed her silence—and perhaps would have drawn a wrong conclusion—had not Monsieur de Clèves returned to end the conversation and visit.

Monsieur de Clèves returned to tell his wife of more news about Sancerre, but she was not interested in the latest developments. She was so preoccupied by what had just taken place that she could hardly hide her state of mental distraction. When she was alone and had time to think, she knew she was entirely wrong in supposing that she had felt nothing more than a passing fancy for Monsieur de Nemours. What he had said had made a deep impression and had convinced her of his love. His actions harmonized too well with his words to leave any doubt. She could no longer entertain the thought that she might not love him. At this time her only thought was how not to give him any indication of her love. It was indeed a difficult task, of which she knew already the pitfalls. She knew the only way of succeeding was to avoid this prince at all costs. Because her mourning period gave her a logical pretext for seclusion, she used it as an excuse not to frequent any more the places where he might see her. She was extremely unhappy and her mother's death seemed to be the cause. No one looked for another.

Monsieur de Nemours was desperate at not seeing her any more, and knowing she was not to be found at any of the gatherings or amusements where the whole court would be assembled, he decided not to be in attendance either. He pretended a great passion for hunting, and arranged hunting parties on the same days the queens were holding court. For a long time a slight illness served as an excuse to stay at home and avoid going to places where he was sure not to find Madame de Clèves.

Monsieur de Clèves about this same time took sick. Madame de Clèves never left his room during his illness, but when he was feeling better and receiving visitors among whom was Monsieur de Nemours, who, on the pretext of being still weak himself, passed there the greater part of each day, she discovered that she dare not remain

in her husband's room any more. The first time Monsieur
de Nemours came she didn't have the strength to leave as
it had been such a long time since she had seen him. This
prince found ways in clever conversation to make her
understand that he was hunting that he might dream, and
avoiding receptions because she was not present. At last,
but with extreme difficulty, she decided to carry out the
resolution of leaving her husband's room whenever Monsieur de Nemours was there. The prince saw that she was
purposely avoiding him and was touched.

At first Monsieur de Clèves took no note of his wife's
conduct, but then he did notice that she never wished to
stay in his room when anyone was there. He spoke to her
about it, and she replied that she did not think it proper
for her to spend every evening in the company of the
younger men of court. She begged him to agree to her
living a more secluded life than the one she had been
living, that the teachings of her mother specified a lot of
things not proper for a young lady of her age to do alone.

Monsieur de Clèves, by nature a kind man, and ordinarily very understanding of his wife, was not so on this
occasion. He told her in no uncertain terms he did not
want to see her conduct change. She was on the verge of
telling him of the rumor at court that Monsieur de Nemours
was in love with her, but she had not the courage.
Besides she felt ashamed to use a false argument and to
veil the real reason from a man who respected her so.

Some days later the king was with the queen at her
hour of receiving. Everyone was speaking of horoscopes
and fortune telling. Opinions were sharply divided on
how much one should rely on them. The queen believed
strongly in them; she maintained, in the light of many
things come true and from what everyone had seen come
to pass, that it was impossible to doubt that there was
some measure of truth in these sciences. Others held that
out of the infinite number of prophecies, so few came
true that quite patently it was all a matter of chance.

"I used to be very inqusitive about the future," said

the king, "but I have been told so many falsehoods and
so many improbabilities that I am convinced no one can
know the truth. Some years ago a man came here reputed to be a great astrologer. Everyone flocked to him;
like the others I went to see him too, but not telling him
who I was. I took along Messieurs de Guise and D'Escars,
whom I made go first. Notwithstanding, the astrologer
first addressed me, as if he knew I was their master.
Perhaps he knew me; however, he told me something
which, if he did know who I was, was not very pleasant
for me to hear. He predicted I would be killed in a duel.
Then he foretold to Monsieur de Guise how he would be
killed from behind, and to D'Escars, that his head would
be smashed by a horse's hoof. Monsieur de Guise was
rather offended since the prophecy seemed to accuse him
of running away from something. Nor was D'Escars exactly pleased to learn that he would end by such an
unfortunate accident. At any rate, we left our astrologer
very unhappy men indeed. I don't know what will happen to Messieurs de Guise and D'Escars, but it doesn't
seem very likely I am going to be killed in a duel. The
King of Spain and I have just concluded the peace, and
had we not come to any peaceful terms, I doubt very
much that we would have resorted to a duel! Or, that I
should have challenged him as my father the king challenged Charles V to a combat of honor."

After this predicted misfortune recounted by the king,
those who had supported the science of astrology abandoned their former position, agreeing that he ought not
give any credence at all to this fantastic story.

"As for me," said Monsieur de Nemours for all to
hear, "I am the one man here who ought least to put any
faith in this science." Then turning to Madame de Clèves,
who was next to him, he whispered, "Someone predicted
that I should be made supremely happy by the kindnesses
and sweet attentions of the person whom I love and
respect the most. You may judge, Madame, if I ought to
believe in prophecies."

Madame la Dauphine, who thought by what Monsieur de Nemours had said aloud that he was telling some false prophecy that had been made to him, asked what he had said to Madame de Clèves. If he had been a man less poised, he would have been surprised by her request, but without hesitation he replied, "I was just telling her, Madame, someone once predicted I was destined for such great heights that I ought not to aspire to them."

Smiling and thinking of his affair in England, Madame replied, "If someone really made this prediction about you, I would advise you not to decry astrology but to search out reasons for supporting it."

Madame de Clèves understood perfectly well what Madame la Dauphine meant, and she also knew that the great things predicted for him did not include being King of England.

Time enough having gone by since the death of her mother, Madame de Clèves decided to make her usual appearances at court. She saw Monsieur de Nemours at Madame la Dauphine's; she met him at her husband's where he often came with other important persons of his own age so as not to be conspicuous. But she never saw him any more without feeling a certain emotional uneasiness, of which he was perfectly aware.

No matter how hard she tried to avoid his glances, to avoid conversation with him more than with any other gentleman, there was something about her movements that made the prince feel for certain she was not indifferent to him. A man less perceptive than he perhaps would not have made this observation. But he had been loved so many times before that it was impossible for him not to recognize the signs. He saw that the Chevalier de Guise was his rival and the chevalier knew that Monsieur de Nemours was his. He was the only man at court to fathom this secret; his own interest in her made him more clairvoyant than others. The knowledge which they had of each other's feelings incited a sort of bitterness between them, which, however, never really broke out

into an open quarrel. But they were opposed in everything. They were always on opposite sides—at racing, at
tilting, at jousting, or at any of the king's amusements.
They could not hide their rivalry.

Madame de Clèves gave much thought to this English
affair; it seemed to her that Monsieur de Nemours could
not very well refuse the advice of the king and the re-
quests of Lignerolles. She saw, much to her chagrin, that
the latter had not yet returned, and she was awaiting
impatiently his arrival. If she could have followed carefully his movements, she would have been better informed about the English affair, but the same sentiments
which aroused her curiosity also forced her to disguise it,
and so she only inquired after the beauty, the character,
the special talents of Queen Elizabeth. Someone brought
a portrait of her to the king, which Madame de Clèves
judged to make the queen appear more beautiful than
she had expected. She could not help but say the picture
was flattering.

"I don't think so," said Madame la Dauphine, who was
there. "This princess is reputed to be very beautiful and
to possess unusual talents. She has been held up to me as
an example all my life. And if she at all resembles her
mother, Anne Boleyn, she must be very charming. Never
was there a lady so attractive in her person and so pleasant in her disposition. I have often heard it said that
there was something distinctive and lively about her face,
and that she was unlike other English beauties."

"Someone told me she was born in France. Is that
true?" questioned Madame de Clèves.

"Those who think so are wrong," replied Madame la
Dauphine. "Let me tell you a short story about her. She
came from a good English family. Henry VIII had been
in love with her sister and her mother; some even thought
that she was his daughter. She came here with the sister
of Henry VII, who married King Louis XII. This princess
was young and carefree, but, after her husband's death,
was very sad at having to leave the French court. But

Anne Boleyn, who was of the same temperament as her mistress, could not decide to go. The late king was in love with her, and she remained at court as a lady-in-waiting to Queen Claude. This queen died, and Madame Marguerite, sister of the king, Duchesse d'Alençon, and afterward, Queen of Navarre, whose stories you have seen, took her into her house. Under the influence of this princess, Anne Boleyn became steeped in the principles of the new religion. Then she went back to England and charmed everyone there with her new learning and French manners. She sang well and danced admirably. She was made a lady-in-waiting to Catherine of Aragon, and King Henry VIII fell madly in love with her.

"Cardinal Wolsey, his favorite and lord chancellor, had aspired to the papacy. Dissatisfied with the emperor because he would not support him in this ambition, Wolsey decided to take revenge by uniting the king his master to the King of France. He put it into Henry VIII's head that his marriage with the emperor's aunt was null and void and suggested to him that he should marry the Duchesse d'Alençon whose husband had just died. Anne Boleyn ambitiously looked upon this divorce as a possible way to the throne. She began to give the King of England ideas about the new religion of Luther, and prevailed upon our late king to favor this divorce in Rome, in the hopes of marrying him to the Duchesse d'Alençon. Cardinal Wolsey, on some other pretexts, fixed it so that he was sent to France to arrange the wedding. But his master would have no part in this scheme. He sent Wolsey orders in Calais that he was not to speak of this marriage.

"On his return from France, Cardinal Wolsey was received with all the honors accorded to a king. Never has a favorite carried pride and vanity to such lengths. He managed a meeting between the two kings at Boulogne. François I extended his hand to Henry VIII who ignored it. Nevertheless, later they entertained each other with lavish magnificence; they exchanged clothing that each had had especially designed for himself. I remember hearing that the suits our late king sent to the King of England were of crimson satin embroidered with triangles of pearls and diamonds and that the robe was of white velvet edged with gold.

"After spending a few days in Boulogne, they went again to Calais. Anne Boleyn was lodged with Henry VIII, with a cortège suitable for a queen, and François I gave her presents and honored her indeed as if she were queen.

"Finally, after a romance that lasted nine years, Henry married her, without waiting for the dissolution of his first marriage which he had long been seeking from Rome. The Pope hastily and abruptly excommunicated him. Henry was so enraged that he declared himself head of the church and dragged all of England into this terrible upheaval in which you see her now. But Anne Boleyn's moment of glory was short-lived. Just when she thought herself comfortably established, after the death of Catherine of Aragon, one day she went with the whole court to the tilting matches to watch her brother, the Lord Rochefort. Here the king became so jealous of her, that, all of a sudden, he left the match and betook himself to London. On arrival he gave orders to arrest the queen, Lord Rochefort, and several others whom he suspected as her lovers or confidants. Although this jealousy seemed to have been born on the spur of the moment, it had been nursed to life by Lady Rochefort, who could not stand the intimacy of her husband with the queen. She made the king see in this relationship an illicit passion. The result was that the king, who was already having an affair with Jane Seymour, now thought only of schemes to be rid of Anne Boleyn. In less than three weeks, he had the queen and her brother tried, their heads lopped off, and he was married to Jane Seymour.

"Later, he had several more wives, whom he discarded or had murdered, among them Catherine Howard, the confidante of Lady Rochefort. They died together. So in the end this lady was punished for crimes she had ascribed to Anne Boleyn. Henry VIII later died, having become quite enormous."

All the ladies who were present at this narration of events by Madame la Dauphine thanked her for informing them so well about the English court, and among them Madame de Clèves, who wanted to know more, particularly about Queen Elizabeth.

The queen-dauphine was having made some miniature portraits of all the court beauties to send to the queen her mother. The day Madame de Clèves' portrait was being finished, Madame la Dauphine came to spend the evening with her. Monsieur de Nemours did not fail to be there. Without letting it become obvious, he never missed an opportunity to see Madame de Clèves. She was so ravishingly beautiful that day that, had he not already been in love with her, he would certainly have fallen for her then. While the artist was painting her portrait, Monsieur de Nemours dared not look at her, for fear that pleasure he derived in gazing at her might be observed.

Madame la Dauphine asked Monsieur de Clèves for a miniature that he had of his wife, to compare it with the one now being painted. Everybody commented on the two portraits. Madame de Clèves asked the artist to touch up the hair-styling of the one they had just brought to her. The artist obeyed, took the picture from its case, worked on it, and put it back on the table.

For a long time Monsieur de Nemours had wanted a portrait of Madame de Clèves. When he saw the one belonging to Monsieur de Clèves, he couldn't resist the urge to steal it from a husband whom he believed to be tenderly loved. Since so many were in the room, he thought he would be no more suspected than anyone else.

Madame la Dauphine was sitting on the bed and was speaking in a low tone with Madame de Clèves, who was standing in front of her. Madame de Clèves could see Monsieur de Nemours through a curtain that was only half drawn; his back was to the table at the foot of the bed; she saw that, without turning his head, he was very cleverly taking something from the table. She knew it must be her portrait, and she was so distressed that Madame la Dauphine noticed she was not paying a bit of attention to what she was saying and she asked her out loud what it was she was looking at. Monsieur de Nemours hearing the question turned around; he met the eyes of Madame de Clèves, who was still staring at him, and he thought that very probably she had seen what he had just done.

Madame de Clèves was most embarrassed. Reason told her that she should ask for her portrait back; yet, if she did this in front of everyone present, it would expose publicly his feelings for her. And yet, if she asked him for it when they were alone, it would encourage him to speak more about his passion. Finally, she judged it was best to let him keep it, and she was happy to accord him this favor without his knowing of her consent.

Monsieur de Nemours noticed her embarrassment, and suspected its cause. He approached her and said softly, "If you saw what I dared to do, please, Madame, would you pretend that you didn't. It is all I dare request of you." Without waiting for her answer, he left.

Madame la Dauphine went out for a walk, followed by all the ladies.

Monsieur de Nemours went to shut himself up at home, not being able to contain in public his delight at owning a portrait of Madame de Clèves. He felt all the joys a man in love could feel. He loved the most charming lady of all the court. He would make her love him in return in spite of herself. He noticed in all her actions a kind of nervousness and hesitation that love causes in youth's first innocence.

That evening, Monsieur de Clèves' household was looking for the portrait everywhere. Since they found its case where it ought to have been, no one suspected that the portrait had been stolen. They thought it had fallen by some accident out of its case. Monsieur de Clèves was disturbed by this loss, and after they had searched everywhere in vain, he said to his wife, but not earnestly, that she undoubtedly had some secret lover to whom she had given this portrait, or who had stolen it, since no one but a lover would have taken the portrait without its case.

These words, said half-jokingly, made a deep impression on Madame de Clèves, and they caused her not a little remorse. She reflected on the violence of the passion that drove her toward Monsieur de Nemours. She found that she had no longer control, either over her words or over the expression on her face. She knew Lignerolles had come back; she realized that she no more feared the affair in England; she was certain that she no longer entertained suspicions about Madame la Dauphine. In a word, she knew there was nothing more to shield her; there was security only in flight. But to flee was not for her to decide. Her predicament was extreme. She felt she had fallen into what seemed to her the greatest of misfortune, namely, letting Monsieur de Nemours see how much she really cared for him. She remembered all Madame de Chartres had said on her deathbed—the advice her mother had given her to take all sorts of precautions, however difficult they might be, rather than to embark on a love affair. Then what Monsieur de Clèves had said about sincerity, when speaking of Madame de Tournon, came to mind. It seemed to her that she ought to confess this attraction for Monsieur de Nemours to her husband. She thought about it for a long time, then was amazed for even thinking about such a foolish idea. She was confused and troubled again because she knew not what to do.

The peace was signed. Princess Élisabeth, in spite of the deep repugnance she felt, decided to obey the king her father. The Duke of Alba, as proxy for Philip of Spain, was appointed to come to marry her; he was soon to arrive. The court was also awaiting the Duc de Savoie, who was coming to marry the king's sister. Both weddings were to take place at the same time. The king was preoccupied with making these weddings a complete success by the amusements he was arranging—amusements that would display the dexterity and magnificence of his court. The best in ballets and plays were proposed as possibilities; the king thought these too private; he wanted something more spectacular. He resolved to have a tournament, open to the foreigners, with the people for spectators. All the princes and young nobles were enthusiastic about this plan of the king's especially the Duke of Ferrara, Monsieur de Guise, and Monsieur de Nemours, all of whom excelled in this kind of sports. The king chose these three to be, along with him, the champions of the tournament.

It was proclaimed throughout the realm, that in the city of Paris, on the fifteenth day of June, His Most Christian Majesty and the princes Alphonse d'Este, Duke of Ferrara, François de Lorraine, Duc de Guise, and Jacques de Savoie, Duc de Nemours shall take on all comers. It was proclaimed that the first combat shall be on horseback in the lists with double armor, four blows of the lance and one for the ladies; that the second combat shall be with swords, one against one or two against two, according to the wishes of the judges; that the third combat on foot, three blows of the halberd and six of the sword; that the champions shall furnish the lances, swords, and halberds chosen by the challengers; that those who cannot control horses shall be disqualified; that there shall be four judges to give the orders, to select the winners, and to decide upon the prizes; that all the challengers, French as well as foreigners, shall be required to touch one or several if they so choose to do; of the shields which shall be hanging on a stack at the end of the lists, where an officer at arms shall be standing to enroll them according to their rank and according to the number of shields they have touched; that three days before the tournament the challengers shall be obliged to have their shield, with arms, brought by a gentleman that it might be hung up; that otherwise they shall not be allowed to participate except by special permission of the champions.

There had been constructed huge lists near the Bastille that extended from the château des Tournelles, crossing the rue Saint-Antoine, to the royal stables. There were two sides of scaffolding and amphitheaters, with covered boxes, which formed kinds of galleries, a very pretty sight, and which could accommodate a large crowd of spectators. All the princes and nobles were busy making necessary preparations. To impress the persons whom they loved, they wanted to appear as brilliantly arrayed as possible.

A few days before the arrival of the Duke of Alba, the king had a tennis match with Monsieur de Nemours, the Chevalier de Guise, and the Vidame de Chartres. The queens, attended by all their ladies, went to watch them. Madame de Clèves was there as well.

After the match, as they were leaving the tennis court, Châtelart approached the queen-dauphine and told her that a love letter, which had fallen out of Monsieur de Nemours' pocket, had just, by chance, been handed to him. The dauphine, who was always curious about what concerned Monsieur de Nemours, asked Châtelart to give it to her. She took it and followed the queen her mother-in-law, who was going with the king to see the work in progress on the lists.

After they had been there some time, the king sent for some horses that had just come. Although they were not yet broken in, the king insisted on their being mounted, and gave one to each of the three gentlemen. The king and Monsieur de Nemours found themselves on the two wildest horses, which wanted to throw themselves at each other. Monsieur de Nemours, for fear of hurting the king, pulled his horse back fiercely and brought it against a pillar of the riding-school, but with such violence that the blow staggered him. Everyone ran to him, thinking he was seriously hurt. Madame de Clèves naturally thought he was more hurt than the others did. The incident caused her much apprehension and concern, which she did not think to conceal. She approached Monsieur de Nemours with the queens, wearing such a changed expression that a man less interested than the Chevalier de Guise could have noticed it. Furthermore, he remarked it because he was far more interested in the condition of Madame de Clèves than in Monsieur de Nemours.

The blow the prince received made him so dizzy that for a long time he remained with bowed head, leaning upon those who were holding him up. When he could finally raise his head, he saw first Madame de Clèves, and on her face he thought he detected a certain compassion. He looked at her in a manner that could only indicate he was moved. Then he thanked the queens for the kindnesses they had shown him, excusing himself for appearing before them in such a state. The king ordered him to go away and rest.

When Madame de Clèves had got over her fright, she soon began to give some thought to the display of anxiety that she might have made. The Chevalier de Guise did not leave her long in the hope that no one had noticed. Giving her his arm to take her from the lists, he said, "I have more reason to complain than Monsieur de Nemours, Madame. You must pardon me if I trespass the bounds of respect I have always had for you, but I must avow a deep hurt over what I have just seen. It is the first time I have been bold enough to speak to you, and indeed it shall be the last. I would rather die or, at least, go into exile, than remain here. To stay is to lose the very sad but consoling thought that all those who set their eyes on you are as wretched as I."

Madame de Clèves could only reply with badly chosen words, as if she had not quite understood what the Chevalier de Guise meant by this statement. Another time she would have taken offense at his speaking of his feelings for her; but now she only felt pained, disturbed, annoyed, that he had recognized for what they were her feelings for Monsieur de Nemours. The Chevalier de

Guise was convinced by her behavior, and so overwhelmed with sorrow that, from that day forward, he resolved never even to think about being loved by Madame de Clèves.

But to leave this situation which had seemed to De Guise a difficult but glorious adventure, he needed some other enterprise, equally as inviting, to occupy his attention. His mind went back to the conquest of Rhodes, to which he had previously given some thought. And when death finally took him from this world, in the flower of his youth and at the height of his princely career, the only regret he had was not having been able to execute his grandiose plan, which he had carefully developed, and the success of which he thought unquestionable.

Madame, leaving the lists, went straight away to the queen, pre-occupied by what had just happened. Monsieur de Nemours came a little later, elegantly attired, like one who had not had an accident at all. He seemed even happier than usual. Joy over what he believed he had seen, gave him an air which enhanced still more his charm. Everybody was surprised when he entered, and everyone went up to him to ask how he was feeling, except Madame de Clèves, who stayed by the mantelpiece, pretending not to see him. The king entered from another room, and seeing him there with the others, called him over to speak more about the accident.

Monsieur de Nemours passed by Madame de Clèves and said very low, "Today I noticed your concern for my well-being, but it is not just your concern that I am most worthy of."

Madame de Clèves had suspected that the prince knew how much she cared for him, and his words just now confirmed her fears. It was terribly tormenting to her to know that she was no longer able to hide her feelings and that the Chevalier de Guise was aware of them also. She was tormented by being definitely aware that Monsieur de Nemours was aware of them, but her torment was not entirely unmixed with a sort of sweetness.

The queen-dauphine, who was extremely anxious to find out what was in the letter Châtelart had given to her, approached Madame de Clèves and said, "Here, go read this letter; it is addressed to Monsieur de Nemours and, from all appearances, it is from this new mistress for whom he has forsaken all the others. If you cannot read it now, keep it and bring it back to me this evening, to my bedroom. Be sure to tell me if you recognize the handwriting."

Having said this, Madame la Dauphine left, and Madame de Clèves was so astonished and in such a state of agitation that for some time she just stood there. Then hurriedly, distraught, she went home, though it was not the usual hour for retiring. Her hand was trembling as she held the letter; her thoughts were jumbled, disturbed, muddled. She found herself in a sort of unbearable pain which never before had she known or experienced. As soon as she was in her room, she opened the letter and read.

LETTER

I have loved you too much to let you believe that the change you detect in me is the result of a silly whim on my part. I want you to know that it is your infidelity which is the cause of it all. You are surprised when I mention your unfaithfulness? You have disguised it so cleverly! And I went to such great pains to keep you from knowing that I knew. You have every reason to be surprised. I am myself surprised that I was able to prevent you from noticing that I knew. Never a sorrow was comparable to mine. I thought you were wildly in love with me. Certainly I was with you. Nor did I conceal my passion for you. Just when I gave you all my heart, I learned that you were deceiving me, that you were in love with another, and quite obviously you were sacrificing me to this new mistress. I knew it the day of the tilting. That is why I didn't go. I feigned illness to hide my mind's disorder. But I did in fact become ill,

*for my body could not support such a violent shock.
When I began to feel well again, I still pretended illness in
order to have a pretext for not seeing you and not writing
to you. I wanted time to decide how best I might deal with
you. Twenty times I made the same resolutions; twenty
times I cast them aside. Finally, I found you unworthy to
be a witness to my sorrow, and I decided that you shouldn't
know of it. I wanted to wound your pride by making you
see that my love was waning. I thought by doing this I
would lessen the price of the sacrifice you were making of
it. I did not want you to have the pleasure of my showing
how much I love you so that you might appear more lovable. I decided to write you lukewarm, listless letters in
order that the person to who you gave them to read would
know I was ceasing to love you. I did not want to accord
this lady the pleasure of knowing by my reproaches and
despair she was triumphing over me. Then I thought, by
simply breaking off relations I would not punish you
enough. Since you did not love me any more, of course,
your pain would be slight. I decided that you must be
forced to love me if you were to feel the anguish of not
being loved, as I most cruelly was. So I thought if there
was anything that could rekindle the love you once had
for me, it was to make you aware that my feelings had
changed—but to do this by pretending to hide it from you
as if I were ashamed to confess it.*

*This I decided upon. But how difficult this decision
was! Seeing you again, how almost impossible to execute!
I was ready a hundred times to burst out in reproaches
and tears. My bad health helped me to hide my troubles
and miseries. I was sustained, too, by the pleasure of
deceiving you, since you were deceiving me. Yet, I did
myself such violence telling and writing to you of my love
that you saw, sooner than I wanted you to, that my feelings had changed. You were duly hurt; you complained. I
tried to reassure you. But my manner was so forced that
you were even more certain that I had ceased to love you.
Finally I accomplished what I set out to do. The fickle-*

ness of your heart made you come back to me, but we had drifted apart. Sweet vengeance was mine! It seemed you loved me better than ever before, and I let you see that my love for you had died. I had reason to believe that you even had abandoned the person from whom I was discarded. I also had very good reasons to believe you had never mentioned my name to her. But neither your return nor polite apologies can repair your fickleness. You have shared your heart with another; you have deceived me. That removes the pleasure of being loved by you, as I thought I deserved. I remain firm in my resolution, which so surprises you, never to see you again.

Madame de Clèves read the letter over and over again, without knowing however what she read. She only knew that Monsieur de Nemours did not love her as she had supposed; that he was in love with some others and was deceiving them as he was deceiving her. What a discovery and revelation for a person of her temperament, so madly in love, who had just laid bare her heart to a man undeserving, who had just mistreated another! Her distress was sharp and intense. It seemed to her that the bitterness of her sorrow was heightened by what had happened during the day; it seemed to her that if Monsieur de Nemour had not led her to believe he loved her, she would not have cared if he had loved another. But she was wrong. The hurt, which she found insufferable, was jealousy with all its attendant horrors. She saw by this letter that Monsieur de Nemours had been carrying on a love affair for a long time. She thought the lady who wrote it was intelligent, distinguished, worthy of being loved; she found in her more courage than she found in herself. She envied the strength she had had to hide her feelings from Monsieur de Nemours. She saw, by the closing, that this person thought she was loved; she concluded that the prince's discreet attitude to herself, by which she had been touched, was perhaps nothing more than the effect of his passion for the other lady whom he feared to displease.

In a word, she thought a thousand black thoughts that only increased her desolation. What remorse! What shame after reflecting on her mother's advice! How she repented not having taken herself away from society, in spite of Monsieur de Clèves' protestations! Now she was sorry she had not told her husband of her attraction to Monsieur de Nemours! She realized too late that it would have been better to have revealed it to a husband of whose kindness she was assured, who would have kept it a secret, than to have revealed it to this man, who was unworthy, who deceived her, who, perhaps, loved her to satisfy his own pride and vanity. All the misfortunes which could happen to her, all the extremities to which she could be driven, were nothing compared to her knowledge that Monsieur de Nemours loved another when she had just disclosed to him her own love for him. Two small consolations were left to her: she had nothing more to fear from herself and she was completely cured of her attraction to this prince.

She scarcely thought of Madame la Dauphine's order to return at bedtime. She went to bed, pretending she wasn't feeling well. When Monsieur de Clèves came back from the king's apartment, he was told she was asleep. But she was far from being in a happy state of repose. She spent the night in misery, rereading the letter.

Madame de Clèves was not the only person whose rest was disturbed by this letter. The Vidame de Chartres, who had lost it—not Monsieur de Nemours—was greatly upset. He had spent the evening with Monsieur de Guise, who had given a dinner for the Duke of Ferrara, his brother-in-law, and for the young people of the court.

By chance, while they were eating, the conversation turned to love letters. The Vidame de Chartres said that he had with him the most beautiful letter that had ever been written. Everyone begged him to show it, but he refused. Monsieur de Nemours teased, saying that he didn't believe the vidame had any such letter at all, that he was only boasting. The vidame replied that he was pushing his discretion to the limit, but all the same he would not show the letter; however, he said he would read certain choice paragraphs, which would convince them that only a few men had ever received such a wonderful letter!

As he was so speaking, he went for the letter, but he could not find it. He searched in vain. They began to joke with him over it. But he appeared so upset about this that they stopped talking to him about it. He left sooner than the others and went hurriedly to his room to see if he had not left it there.

While he was still looking for the letter, the first valet of the queen, sent by the Vicomtesse d'Uzès, came to him to apprise him of what they were saying at the queen's.

Apparently a love letter had dropped from the vidame's pocket while he was playing tennis. Someone had divulged a great part of its contents, and the queen was very much interested in it. She had sent one of her servants to fetch it, and he had told her that he gave it to Châtelart. Furthermore, the first valet told the Vidame de Chartres many other things besides, which caused him much anxiety.

The valet left instantly to go to a close friend of Châtelart. He got him out of bed, although it was a ridiculous hour to go looking for a letter, not telling him who wanted the letter or who had lost it.

Châtelart, who had made up his mind that it belonged to Monsieur de Nemours and that this prince was in love with Madame la Dauphine, did not doubt that it was he who was asking for it. He answered, with a touch of malicious pleasure, that he had given the letter to the queen-dauphine.

The gentleman went back to the Vidame de Chartres with this reply. And more than ever the vidame was unnerved. For a long time he was undecided what he should do. Finally, he thought that the only person who could help him out of this mess was Monsieur de Nemours.

He went to him and entered his room just about dawn. The prince was sleeping peacefully; what he had seen of Madame de Clèves the day before had induced nothing but sweet thoughts. He was surprised to be so rudely awakened by the Vidame de Chartres. He asked him why he had come to disturb his sleep? Was it to take revenge on him for what he had said during dinner? But then he saw by the expression on the vidame's face that a serious matter brought him there at that hour.

"I come to entrust you with the most important business of my life," the vidame said to de Nemours. "I know you won't like me for this, but I need your help desperately. I know that I would have lost your respect if I had told you what I am about to say without being constrained by necessity to do so. I dropped this letter that I told you about last evening. It is of the utmost importance that no one know that it is addressed to me. I dropped it on the tennis court yesterday, and a lot of people who were there have seen it. You were there too and I beg you, please, say it was you who lost it."

"You must think that I don't have a mistress," said Monsieur de Nemours with a smile, "to make me such a proposition. Do you imagine that I have a mistress who would not misunderstand if I allowed her to think I received such letters?"

"I beg you," said the vidame, "listen to me seriously. If you have a mistress, as I don't doubt, though I have no idea who she is, it would be easy for you to explain it away and I shall give you some infallible means. Even if you would not be able to explain, it would only cost you a short misunderstanding. But I, by this accident, dishonor a person who has passionately loved me, who is one of the finest ladies in the world. Furthermore, I shall bring upon myself an implacable hatred which shall cost me my everlasting fortune and perhaps more besides."

"I cannot understand everything you are saying," replied Monsieur de Nemours, "but you make me suspect that some rumors I hear concerning a certain great princess being very much interested in you, are not without foundation."

"They are not true," shot back the Vidame de Chartres. "Would to God they were, I would not be in the mess I am. But I must tell you everything to make you see what I have to fear.

"Every since I have been at court, the queen has always treated me very kindly and pleasantly, and I have had every reason to believe she was actually a little fond of me, although I can't exactly say why. For her I have had no other sentiments but those of deepest respect. I was even in love at the time with Madame de Thémines. You only have to see her to realize how easy it would be to fall in love with her.

"Nearly two years ago when the court was at Fontainebleau, I found myself on two or three occasions in conversation with the queen—at times with very few people around. We had mutual interests and we readily agreed with each other's opinions.

"One day, among other things, we began to speak about trusting people. I said there was no one whom I trusted completely, because, having done so, I always regretted it later. But, I said, I knew a lot of things which I kept secret. The queen told me she esteemed me more for this. She went on to say that she had never found anyone in France who could keep a secret and that this was most distressing to her, since it robbed one of the pleasure of telling secrets; that, in life, it was necessary to have someone in whom one could confide, particularly for a person in her station.

"On the following days, she pursued again the same topic of conversation, even telling me of some rather confidential matters that were going on.

"At last, it occurred to me she wanted to exchange confidences. This thought attracted me to her, and I was touched that she should pay me this distinction. I began to give her much more attention than I was accustomed to.

"One evening when the king and all the ladies went riding in the forest (she didn't go because she was not feeling well) I stayed behind with her. She went down to the pond's bank, leaving her equerries so she could walk alone. She walked around for a while, then approached and beckoned me to follow her.

" 'I would like to speak with you,' she said, 'and you shall see presently, by what I have to say, that I am one of your friends.'

"She stopped at these words and stared at me. Then she continued, 'You are in love, and because you confide in no one, you suppose your love is not known. But it is known, and even by interested people. You are closely watched, the place where you meet your mistress is known, plans are in the offing to surprise you there. I do not know who she is, I do not ask you to tell me, I only want to protect you from the trap you are falling into.'

"Observe, I beg you, what trap this queen was setting for me and how difficult it was for me not to be caught in it. She wished to know if I was in love. And by not asking me pointed questions, and by letting me see she was only interested in my well-being, she took me unawares.

"However, against all appearances, I got to the truth. I was in love with Madame de Thémines; but although she loved me, I was not fortunate enough to have secret trysting places where I feared being surprised, and thus I surmised it wasn't she of whom the queen was speaking. I also knew that I was having another affair with a woman who was less beautiful and less virtuous than Madame de Thémines, and that it was not possible for anyone to know where we carried on our rendezvous. But since I cared little for her, it was easy to protect myself from this sort of danger by simply not seeing her.

"So I decided that I would tell the queen nothing, that, on the contrary, I would tell her that a long time ago, I had abandoned all hope of ever falling in love with the kind of woman I wanted.

" 'You are not being sincere with me,' said the queen. 'Just the contrary of what you are saying is the truth. The manner in which I have spoken to you ought to oblige you not to conceal anything from me. I want to be your friend,' she continued, 'but you must not conceal any of your attachments from me. If you want my friendship, you have my price. I will give you two days to think about it, but after that time, think before you tell me anything—and remember, if, later on, I find you have deceived me, I shall never forgive you.'

"The queen left me without waiting for my answer. You can imagine how I pondered what she had just said. The two days she had given me to make up my mind did not seem any too long. I saw that she wished to know if I were in love, and she didn't want me to be. I saw immediately the consequences and the probable aftermath of the decision I was going to make. My vanity was not a little flattered at the possibility of a liaison with a queen, and a queen at that who was still extremely beautiful. On the other hand, I loved Madame de Thémines, and although I was in a way being unfaithful to her with this other woman I mentioned, I could not break with this woman. I saw the danger in which I was placing myself by deceiving the queen, a most difficult person to fool. Yet I could not decide to refuse what fortune was offering me. I ran the risk of what my bad behavior might effect, and broke relations with this woman whose identity might be discovered. I was hoping to hide my love for Madame de Thémines.

"At the end of two days, as I went into the queen's room where all the ladies were assembled, she said to me out loud with a serious air that surprised me, 'Have you thought about the business which I asked you to consider? What is the truth?'

"Yes, Madame, I answered. It is just as I told you, your majesty.

" 'Come this evening at letter-writing time, she replied, 'and I shall give you further instructions.'

"I made a profound bow without saying a word, and I did not fail to be present at the designated hour. I found her in the gallery where her desk was, attended by her ladies. As soon as she saw me, she came over to me, and led me to the other end of the room.

" 'Well,' she said, 'upon due reflection you have nothing to say to me even after the manner in which I spoke to you? Does that not merit a little more frankness on your part?'

"I am speaking to you sincerely, Madame. That is why I have nothing to tell you. And I swear to your majesty with all the respect I owe, that I am not in love with any lady of this court.

" 'I want to believe it,' said the queen, 'because I wish it, and I wish it because I want you to give yourself entirely to me. If you were in love, it would be impossible for me to be happy with your friendship. Lovers cannot be trusted; one cannot depend upon them. They are too distracted, too divided, and too preoccupied with their mistresses. I don't want this kind of a relationship. Remember that it is because of your word that you are uncommitted that I have chosen you in whom to place all my confidences. You are to have no friend, male or female, of whom I shall not approve. Your sole preoccupation must be to please me. I shall take good care of your fortunes; I shall watch over them with more attention than you yourself would give them. Whatever I am able to do for you will be my pleasure and my reward.

" 'I have chosen you in whom to confide all my problems and troubles. You will help me soften their hurt. I seem to suffer without a lot of pain the king's attachment to the Duchesse de Valentinois; but it is unbearable. She governs the king, she deceives him, she despises me, and all my people are on her side. The queen my daughter-in-law, proud of her beauty and the prestige of her uncles, pays me no respect. The Connétable de Montmorency is the real master of the king and the kingdom. He hates me and has shown his hatred in ways I can't forget. The Maréchal of Saint-André is a young, audacious favorite who doesn't treat me any better than the rest. The details of my sorrows would make you pity me. I dared not until this moment tell anyone, but I trust you. See to it you do not betray my trust. You are my only consolation.'

"As she finished her eyes reddened. I was so deeply moved by her kindness I wanted to hurl myself at her feet. Ever since that day she has put her complete trust in me. She does nothing without first consulting me. Our relationship exists thus to this very day."

BOOK III

꙰

"Nevertheless, no matter how distraught and preoccupied I was with this new intimacy with the queen, I still clung to Madame de Thémines, whose attraction I could not resist. It seemed she had stopped loving me. Hence, if I had been wise, I would have used this change in her heart to cure me of my love for her. Instead, my love redoubled. I acted so indiscreetly that the queen became aware of my secret attachment. Jealousy is quite natural in persons of her nationality, and perhaps this princess did have feelings for me stronger than she realized herself. Well, anyway, the rumor that I was in love so upset her and so troubled her that I thought, a hundred times, that as far as she was concerned I was through. Finally, I reassured her by my little attentions, by my submissions, by my false vows; but I would not have been able to deceive her for long had not the change in Madame de Thémines driven us apart in spite of my efforts to hold her affection as well as the queen's. She made me see that she loved me no more. And I was so sure of this that I was constrained not to torment her further but to leave her in peace. Sometime later she wrote this letter to me which I lost. I realized by this letter that she knew of my intimacy with this other woman, of whom I spoke to you, and that this was the reason for the change in her affection.

"Since I had nothing then which divided my interest,

the queen was quite satisfied with me. But since the feelings I had for her were not of such a nature as to make me incapable of all other attachments, and since one does not fall in love of his own volition, I fell in love at this time with Madame de Martigues, for whom I had had some feeling when she was a Villemontais, and an attendant of the queen-dauphine. I had reason to believe she didn't exactly hate me either. My discretion in this affair, for which she does not know the reasons, pleases her immensely. The queen doesn't suspect anything. But she is suspicious of something else no less annoying. As Madame de Martigues is always with the queen-dauphine, I also go to see the queen-dauphine much more often than usual. The queen imagines that it is this princess with whom I am in love. The position of the queen-dauphine, which is equal to that of the queen's, and her beauty and youthfulness, which are superior to the queen's, have made the queen so furiously jealous and so spiteful toward her daughter-in-law that she can no longer conceal it. The Cardinal de Lorraine, who, for a long time now, seems to me to have courted the good graces of the queen, and who sees that I occupy the place in her heart that he should like to have, has, under the pretext of resolving the differences between these two queens, now entered the affair. I don't doubt that he has unraveled the cause of the queen's bitterness and that, in fact, he is doing me all sorts of bad turns without letting the queen know his ulterior motives.

"This is the state of affairs as they stand with me now. Imagine what this lost letter might cost me. I put it in my pocket to return it to Madame de Thémines. If the queen should see this letter, she will know at once I have deceived her; she will know too that while I was deceiving her for Madame de Thémines, I was being unfaithful to Madame de Thémines also. Can you imagine what she will think of me? Can you imagine her ever trusting me again? If she doesn't see this letter at all, what shall I say to her? She knows someone gave the letter to Madame la

Dauphine; she will jump to the conclusion that Châtelart recognized the handwriting of this queen and that the letter is from her; she will fancy that the jealous person alluded to in the letter is herself. She will think a thousand and one black thoughts, and I stand to lose on all of them. And, furthermore, add to all this that I am in love with Madame de Martigues and that Madame la Dauphine will surely show the letter to her, which she will certainly judge to have been written recently. Thus, I shall be in a terrible muddle, both with the person whom I love most and with the person whom I fear most.

"You see why I implore you to say that the letter is yours. You see why I ask you, please, go and get the letter from Madame la Dauphine."

"I see," said Monsieur de Nemours, "you are in a predicament. But I must say you deserve it. And they accuse me of being unfaithful and having too many affairs going at once! But you surpass me, my friend! I should never have dared to do what you have done. How could you aspire to keep Madame de Thémines and to involved yourself with the queen? And how could you even hope to keep the queen and deceive her? She is the queen and Italian—consequently, full of suspicions, full of jealousy, and full of pride. *Mon Dieu!* When, by your good luck, rather than by your finesse, you extricate yourself from these entanglements, what do you do? You take on new ones, and you fancy that, in the midst of the court, you could love Madame de Martigues without the queen becoming aware of it! The queen is violently in love with you, discretion prevents you from confessing it. My discretion prevents me from asking if she loves you. She is now suspicious, and the truth is against you."

"Look, must you reprimand me?" interrupted the vidame. "Your experience in situations of this kind ought to make you more indulgent of my errors. I readily admit I am wrong, but, please, I beg you, try to help me out of this abysmal mess. It seems to me you could see the queen-dauphine as soon as she is awakened to ask for this letter back as though it was you who had lost it."

"I have already told you," replied Monsieur de Nemours, "that this proposition of yours is a bit fantastic and, in my particular situation, not without its difficulties. Furthermore, if they saw the letter fall from your pocket, it would be rather foolish of me to expect them to believe it fell from mine."

"I thought I had mentioned," replied the vidame, "that they told the queen-dauphine that it fell from your pocket."

"What!" said Monsieur de Nemours brusquely, who saw immediately in what a bad light this letter could cast him with Madame de Clèves. "You mean the queen-dauphine was told that it was I who dropped this letter?"

"Yes, that is what they told her," answered the vidame. "And what caused this misunderstanding was that there were several gentlemen servants of both queens in the gaming room when your servants and mine went to get our wraps. At this time the letter was dropped. The servants picked it up and read it aloud. Some thought it was yours, and some of the others, mine. Châtelart, who took it and whom I have just asked for it, says that he gave it to the queen-dauphine as a letter belonging to you. Those who spoke about it to the queen unfortunately said that it was mine. Hence, you can easily do what I ask and get me out of this predicament."

Monsieur de Nemours had always been rather fond of the Vidame de Chartres whose relationship to Madame de Clèves made him even dearer to Monsieur de Nemours. Nevertheless, he could not risk the chance that Madame de Clèves might hear of the letter and associate his name with it. He set to thinking about it and the vidame, guessing almost exactly what was on his mind, said:

"It is obvious you fear a misunderstanding with your mistress. You would even lead me to believe your mistress is the queen-dauphine. That I could believe, were it not for the fact Monsieur d'Anville shows little jealousy toward you. But, whoever she is, it isn't fair that you should sacrifice your peace of mind for mine, and I shall make it clear to the lady whom you love that the letter was addressed to me and not to you. Here is a note from Madame d'Amboise, a close friend of Madame de Thémines in whom she has confided all her secrets of affection for me. In this letter Madame d'Amboise asks me to return the letter I have lost. My name is on the note, and its contents prove beyond a shadow of a doubt that the letter that they are asking for is the same one that has been found. I will leave this note with you, and you have my permission to show it to your mistress for justification. I beg you not to lose a moment, but to go this very morning and see Madame la Dauphine."

Monsieur de Nemours promised the vidame to do what he asked and took Madame d'Amboise's note; but he decided not to see the queen-dauphine first—he had more urgent business to do. He had no doubt that the queen-dauphine had already spoken about this letter to Madame de Clèves, and he couldn't bear that a person whom he loved so much could entertain for a moment the idea that he was involved with another woman.

So he went to Madame de Clèves' apartment when he thought she might be awake and had someone inform her that only a matter of extreme importance obliged him to ask for an interview at such an extraordinary hour. Madame de Clèves was still in bed, terribly upset by the sad thoughts that had kept her awake all night long. She was extremely surprised by this unexpected visit of Monsieur de Nemours. But so bitter was she that, without hesitation, she sent word she was sick and did not wish to speak to him.

The prince was not annoyed by her refusal. On the contrary, a show of coldness, at a time when she could be jealous, was not a bad sign. He went to Monsieur de Clèves' room, and told him that he had just come from his wife's room, that he was sorry to be unable to see her since he had something important to tell her concerning the Vidame de Chartres. In a few words he conveyed to

Monsieur de Clèves the substance of his business, who afterward took him straight away to his wife's room. If she had not been in the dark, she would scarcely have been able to conceal agitation and surprise at seeing Monsieur de Nemours enter her bedroom, led by her husband. Monsieur de Clèves told her it was about a letter, concerning which, in the interests of the vidame, her help was needed, that she was to discuss with Monsieur de Nemours what had to be done, that, as for him, he was off to see the king who had just sent for him.

Monsieur de Nemours was now alone with Madame de Clèves just as he wanted to be. "I have come to ask you, Madame," he said, "if Madame la Dauphine has not spoken to you about a certain letter which Châtelart gave to her yesterday."

"She said something about it," replied Madame de Clèves. "But I hardly see what this letter has to do with my uncle. I can assure you his name isn't mentioned in it."

"That is true, Madame. His name is not mentioned," said Monsieur de Nemours. "But the letter is addressed to him, and it is of utmost importance to him that you should get it back from Madame la Dauphine."

"It is difficult for me to understand," replied Madame de Clèves, "why he is so concerned that the letter is seen and why he is asking for the letter to be returned."

"If you will be good enough to listen, Madame, I will explain it all and try to show you in what way this matter is of such importance to the vidame. I would not have told Monsieur de Clèves had I not needed his help to have the honor of seeing you."

"Everything you have to say is quite useless," replied Madame de Clèves with an air of cold indifference. "I think it would be better for you to go yourself to the queen-dauphine, and to tell her, with no apologies, the interest you have in this letter, because, as a matter of fact, she has been told the letter is yours."

Monsieur de Nemours, more pleasurably aware of Madame de Clèves' bitter frame of mind than he had ever been, was reluctant to justify himself.

"I do not know, Madame," he said, "what could have been told to Madame la Dauphine, but this letter has nothing to do with me. Furthermore, it is addressed unmistakably to Monsieur le Vidame."

"I believe you," replied Madame de Clèves. "But someone has told the queen-dauphine just the contrary, and it will not seem logical to her that these letters should fall from your pocket. That is why, unless you have some other reason, of which I am unaware, for hiding the truth from her, I would advise you to own up to it."

"I have nothing to own up to; the letter is not mine. If there is anyone whom I should want to convince, it certainly is not the Madame la Dauphine. But, Madame, as it is of great importance to Monsieur le Vidame, please be good enough to let me tell you some things which you ought to know."

Madame de Clèves, by her silence, indicated she was ready to hear him out. As succinctly as he possibly could, he narrated all that he had just learned from the vidame. What he said caused Madame de Clèves much astonishment. But although she listened attentively, she remained cold, so as to give the impression either that she didn't believe the story to be true or that she was totally indifferent to it. Her mind was closed until Monsieur de Nemours mentioned to her the note from Madame d'Amboise, addressed to the Vidame de Chartres, which was the proof of everything that he had just told her. Because Madame de Clèves knew that this woman was Madame de Thémines' friend, she found a semblance of truth in what Monsieur de Nemours was saying. Perhaps the letter was not addressed to him after all. Suddenly, and in spite of herself, she was no longer cold and indifferent to his story. Monsieur de Nemours, having read the letter to her, offered it to her and said she could probably recognize the handwriting. She could not help taking it and looked at the top of it to see if it were addressed to the Vidame de Chartres. She read it in its entirety to judge if indeed the letter she had was the same they were asking for. Monsieur de Nemours said everything he could to convince her, and since we believe easily what we want to believe, he satisfied Madame de Clèves that the letter had nothing at all to do with him.

She then began to discuss with Monsieur de Nemours the vidame's predicament and danger, at first blaming him for his naughty conduct, then looking for ways to help him. She was astonished at the queen's behavior. She confessed to Monsieur de Nemours that she had the letter in her possession. Finally, as soon as she believed him innocent, she entered with an open and composed frame of mind into the things which at first did not seem to merit her credence. They agreed that it was not necessary to return the letter to the queen-dauphine for fear she might show it to Madame de Martigues who knew the handwriting of Madame de Thémines and who would have easily guessed, by the great interest she took in the Vidame, that the letter was addressed to him. They also decided not to say anything to the queen-dauphine about the queen, her mother-in-law. Madame de Clèves, on the pretext she was acting in her uncle's interests, agreed most willingly to keep all that Monsieur de Nemours had said a secret.

This prince did not spend all his time talking about the vidame's affairs. The liberty he enjoyed during this interview would have given him a boldness that he had not up to this point dared to take, if someone had not come to inform Madame de Clèves that the queen-dauphine was requesting her presence immediately.

Monsieur de Nemours had to leave. He went to find the vidame to tell him that after leaving him, he deemed it more in their interests to go to Madame de Clèves, who was his niece, than to go straight to the queen-dauphine. He was not without sound reasons to make the vidame approve of his actions, and he gave him every indication that everything would turn out well.

Madame de Clèves dressed quickly to go to the queen-dauphine. Hardly had she arrived when this princess made her approach and said softly:

"I have been waiting two hours for you, and never have I had so much difficulty in hiding the truth as I have had this morning. The queen has heard some talk about the letter I gave you yesterday; she thinks it is the Vidame de Chartres who dropped it. You know she is very much interested in him. She is looking for this letter; in fact, she has already sent someone to Châtelart asking for it. He said he had given it to me. So they have been here, asking for it, under the pretext it was a cute little letter about which the queen was not a little curious. I dared not say that you had it; she would have imagined that I gave it to you because of the vidame being your uncle and that there was some understanding between him and me. I have already remarked how jealous she is when he is with me too frequently. So I told her the letter was in the dress I was wearing yesterday and that those who had the key to my wardrobe had already left. Please, Madame," she added, "give me the letter right away so I can send it to her. But first, let me read it before sending it to see if I can recognize the handwriting."

Madame de Clèves was more embarrassed than she had thought possible. "I don't know," she said, "what you can do, Madame, but Monsieur de Clèves, to whom I gave the letter to read, returned it to Monsieur de Nemours, who came this morning, imploring us to get it back from you. Monsieur de Cléves was imprudent enough to tell him he had it and had the weakness to give in to his request."

"You have put me in a most embarrassing situation," replied Madame la Dauphine, "and you were entirely wrong to give this letter to Monsieur de Nemours without my permission since it was I who gave you this letter. Now what am I to say to the queen, and what is she going to think? She will imagine, and quite rightly, that this letter concerns me, and that there is something going on between me and the vidame. Never will she be convinced that it belongs to Monsieur de Nemours."

"I am very sorry for putting you in this awkward position," answered Madame de Clèves. "It is very serious. But really, it is my husband's fault and not mine."

"It's your fault for having given him the letter," retorted the dauphine. "No other woman in the world tells all she knows to her husband."

"I know that I am wrong, Madame," said Madame de Clèves. "But let's think how we might repair the fault, instead of examining whose fault it was."

"Do you remember at all what was in the letter?" asked the queen-dauphine.

"Yes, Madame, I do remember, having read it several times."

"In that case," replied Madame la Dauphine, "you must go at once and rewrite it in a disguised handwriting. And I will then send that one to the queen. She will not show it to the people who have already seen it. If she does, I will maintain it's the one Châtelart gave me, and he won't dare deny it."

Madame de Clèves agreed to this expedient. She thought that she would send for Monsieur de Nemours in order that she might see the real letter again. Thus she could copy it word for word and imitate the handwriting as closely as she could. She thought that the queen would be completely fooled by this.

As soon as she was home, she told her husband of Madame la Dauphine's dire situation, and begged him to send for Monsieur de Nemours, which he did. He came with all possible dispatch. Madame de Clèves told him all she had already told her husband, and then asked him for the letter. But Monsieur de Nemours replied that he had already given it back to the Vidame de Chartres, who was so overjoyed to have it in his possession again and to find himself out of danger that he sent it immediately to Madame de Thémines' friend.

Madame de Clèves was in a new embarrassing posi-

tion. At last, after much discussion and thinking, they
decided to write the letter from memory. They shut themselves up to work on it, leaving explicit orders with the
servants that they were not to be disturbed and sending
all of Monsieur de Nemours' people away. This situation
of mystery and intrigue was not without its charm for the
prince, and even for Madame de Clèves. Her scruples in
some way were resolved by the presence of her husband
and the fact they were working in the interests of the
vidame. She felt only an exhilarating joy and pleasure
never experienced before because she was seeing Monsieur de Nemours again. And this joy, carefree and play-
ful, which Monsieur de Nemours had never before noticed
in her, increased a hundredfold his love. Since he also
had never spent such pleasurable moments with her, his
vivacity sparkled, and whenever Madame de Clèves would
begin remembering about the letter and how to write it,
this prince, instead of seriously helping her, did nothing
but interrupt and jest with her. Madame de Clèves slipped
into this same spirit of levity so that, after they had been
working on the letter for a long time and Madame la
Dauphine had sent messengers twice to tell Madame de
Clèves to hurry, they had not yet completed half the
letter.

Monsieur de Nemours was delighted to stretch these
pleasant hours, and he quite forgot about the interests of
his friend the vidame. Madame de Clèves was not bored
either, and she too forgot the interests of her uncle.

Finally, at four o'clock the letter was hurriedly finished, but so badly written and the handwriting so ineptly
imitated that the queen could hardly fail to surmise the
real truth of the matter. And she was not deceived by it.
No matter what was said to try to convince her that the
letter was written to Monsieur de Nemours, she was
certain, not only that it belonged to the Vidame de
Chartres, but also that the queen-dauphine had something to do with it and that there was some relationship

between them. This thought intensified her hate for the princess. The queen never forgave the queen-dauphine and persecuted her until at last she was constrained to leave France.

As for the Vidame de Chartres, he was ruined in the queen's eyes. Whether the Cardinal de Lorraine had had any influence over her, or whether the episode of this letter helped her to unravel other deceptions the vidame had practiced, it is certain the rift between them was never bridged. Their liaison ended, and she effected his final ruin at the time of the Amboise conspiracy in which he was involved.

After they had sent the letter to Madame la Dauphine, Monsieur de Clèves and Monsieur de Nemours left. Madame de Clèves remained alone. As soon as she was no longer buoyed up by that special feeling of happiness that the presence of one's lover gives, she came back to her senses, as if from a dream. She looked, with surprise, at the remarkable difference between her present state of mind and that of the evening before; she reviewed the coldness and bitterness she had displayed to Monsieur de Nemours, supposing Madame de Thémines' letter was addressed to him. And now what calm! What sweet delight to know for sure the letter didn't concern him! When she reflected that, on the day before, she had reproached herself for having revealed her affection for him, which was really only ordinary compassion, and that, now, by her bitterness, she had disclosed to him feelings of jealousy, which are certain unmistakable signs of love, she could no more recognize herself. When she reflected more that Monsieur de Nemours took note of her love for him, that, in spite of his certain knowledge of it, she did not treat him any the worse for it, even in the presence of her husband, but that, on the contrary, she had never looked upon him so favorably, and that she was even the cause of Monsieur de Clèves' sending for him and arranging their afternoon together, she knew that she had embarked on some relationship with Monsieur de Nemours. She knew that she was deceiving her husband who merited least of all to be deceived. And, too, she felt ashamed to appear so little worthy of esteem in the eyes of her lover. But what she could bear least of all was the memory of the bitter state of her mind the evening before when she had supposed Monsieur de Nemours was in love with another and was flagrantly deceiving her.

Till now she had been ignorant of the deadly anguish caused by suspicion and jealousy. She had only thought of warding off her love for Monsieur de Nemours. She had not yet begun to fear that he might be in love with another. Although the suspicions, caused by this letter, had been effaced, they opened her eyes to an emotion she had never before experienced—jealousy. She was astounded at her own naiveté in not realizing how unlikely it was that a man like Monsieur de Nemours, who had always seemed to be so fickle with women, would be capable of any sincere and lasting attachment. She felt it was almost impossible to be happy with his kind of love.

"But even if I could be happy," she said to herself, "what would I do with it? Do I wish to have it? Do I wish to reciprocate it? Do I want to get involved in this love affair? Do I want to be unfaithful to Monsieur de Clèves? Do I want to be unfaithful to myself? Do I want really to expose myself to love's cruel regrets and tears? I am overwhelmed and vanquished by this infatuation which drags me on in spite of myself. All my resolutions are vain. I thought yesterday all these thoughts of today; but I am doing today the exact opposite of what yesterday I resolved not to do. I must remove myself from his presence. I must go to the country, no matter how strange this trip might appear to everybody—and if Monsieur de Clèves is dead set against it and wants me to offer reasons for going, perhaps I shall hurt him and myself by telling him quite frankly."

She was firm in her resolution and remained at home the whole evening without going to the dauphine's to find out what had happened over the forged letter.

When Monsieur de Clèves returned, she told him she wanted to go to the country. She said that she was feeling ill and had need of country air. Monsieur de Clèves, thinking that her obvious freshness and beauty in no way indicated any serious illness, at first laughed at her proposed trip and said that she was forgetting the marriage ceremonies of the princesses and the tournament about to take place. He said that she didn't have too much time to get herself ready if she were to make her appearance with the same magnificence as the other ladies. But her husband's reasons could not change her mind, and she begged him to please let her go to Coulommiers while he went with the king to Compiègne. Coulommiers was a beautiful house, a day's journey from Paris, which they were building. Monsieur de Clèves finally consented. So she went, not planning to return in the near future. The king left for Compiègne where he was to be only for a few days.

Monsieur de Nemours had not seen Madame de Clèves since that very pleasant afternoon, which had done so much to raise his hopes. He was restless and impatient to see her again, so that when the king returned to Paris, he decided to go see his sister, the Duchesse de Mercoeur, who lived in the country rather close by Coulommiers. He suggested to the vidame that he should accompany him there in the hope that, with the vidame, a visit to Madame de Clèves might more easily be arranged. The vidame willingly accepted the invitation.

Madame de Mercoeur welcomed them joyfully and thought only of entertaining them and making their visit to the country an enjoyable experience. One day while they were deer hunting, Monsieur de Nemours found himself lost in the forest; and asking for directions back, he discovered he was in the vicinity of Coulommiers. At the mention of the word Coulommiers, without any reflection and with no plans, he galloped off at full speed in the direction that was indicated to him. He found himself deep in the forest, wandering about haphazardly on well-kept paths that he judged led to the château. At the end of one of these paths, he came upon a pavilion whose lower floor consisted of one large salon, with two adjoining alcoves, one of which opened out onto a flower garden, separated from the forest only by a fence, and the other looked down a vista that trailed into the park. He entered the pavilion and would have stopped to admire the beauty around him had he not seen Monsieur and Madame de Clèves coming up this pathway accompanied by their servants. As he had not expected to find Monsieur de Clèves, whom he thought he had left with the king, his first impulse was to hide. He went into the little alcove that overlooked the flower garden, hoping to leave by a door which opened into the forest. But seeing that Madame de Clèves and her husband were seated in the garden, that their servants stayed in the park, and that he could not exit without Monsieur and Madame de Clèves noticing, he could not deny himself the pleasure of gazing upon this princess nor could he resist the curiosity to listen to her conversation with her husband who now incited more jealousy than any of his rivals.

He overheard what Monsieur de Clèves was saying to his wife: "But why don't you want to come back to Paris? What is there to keep you here in the country? For some time now, your frenzy for solitude has surprised me and disturbed me because it separates us. I even find you more depressed than usual, and I fear you are worrying over some thing or other."

"No, there is nothing wrong," she replied, rather embarrassed. "But the tumult at court, the frequent visitors at home, and the constant upheaval weary me, body and soul. I need rest."

"Rest," he replied, "is scarcely for a person of your age. You are at ease at court. This ought not to weary you. I fear rather, my dear, that you don't mind our separation at all."

"If you think that, you are being unfair to me," she replied with growing embarrassment. "I beg you to leave me here. If you could stay too with me, without all these people who never seem to leave your side, I should be extremely happy."

"Ah! Madame," cried Monsieur de Clèves, "your demeanor and your words make me see you have reasons of which I am unaware for staying by yourself. What are they?"

He pressed her for a long time, unsuccessfully, to tell her reasons. She defended her position, however, in such a way that her husband's curiosity was considerably aroused. For a long minute there was silence, her eyes were cast down. Suddenly, looking up at him, she said: "Do not force me to confess something which I do not have the courage to confess, although for a long time I have often wanted to. But just try to realize that it is not prudent for a woman of my age, who desires to be mistress of her behavior, to be exposed to the society of the court."

"The pictures you are painting in my mind, Madame," cried out Monsieur de Clèves, "I would not dare to describe for fear of offending you."

Madame de Clèves did not answer; her silence confirmed what her husband had dared only to think.

"You are saying nothing," he continued, "and by your silence you tell me my thoughts are correct."

"All right," she cried, throwing herself on her knees. "I am going to make a confession such as no woman has ever made to her husband before. Only the innocence of my conduct and my good intentions now give me strength and courage. It is true I have my reasons for leaving the court. It is true that I want to avoid perils into which young women of my age sometimes fall. I have never given any sign of weakness, nor should I fear to give any, if you would allow me to stay away from court or if I had still Madame de Chartres to help me. However dangerous is the decision I am now making, I make it with joy that I might prove myself worthy of you. If my sentiments are distasteful to you, I ask you a thousand pardons. At least I shall never displease you by my actions. Only consider that to do what I am doing attests my deep affection and profound esteem for you. Help me, have pity on me, and love me still if you can."

Monsieur de Clèves remained, while she spoke, with his head in his hands, beside himself with grief, and he had not thought to lift her up. When she finished, and he saw her on her knees, her face bathed in tears, so admirably beautiful, he thought he would die of sorrow. He lifted her up and kissed her.

"You, Madame, have pity on me," he said to her. "I am worthy of it, and excuse me if in the first moments of a terrible sorrow, I have not responded as I should to a trial such as yours! You seem to me more worthy of my esteem and admiration than all the other women in the world; but then too I am the most wretched man ever born. I have loved you from the very first moment I laid eyes on you. Your coldness and the possession of you could not extinguish the fire of my love. It burns even now. But I have never been able to pierce you with my love, and now I see you are afraid of loving another. Who is he, Madame, this lucky man who inspires your fear? Since when has he attracted you? What has he done to win your heart? What road did he discover to find your love? I consoled myself in some fashion thinking that, since I was incapable of touching your heart, no one could. Now another has done what I have been unable to do. I am both a jealous husband and a jealous lover; but it is impossible for me to be a jealous husband after a trial such as yours. It is too noble not to give me complete confidence in you. It consoles me even as your lover. Your confidence and frankness are of inestimable value. You respect me enough to believe I will not abuse this trust. You are right, Madame, I shall neither abuse it nor love you any the less for it. You have made me unhappy only by the greatest proof of fidelity that a woman could ever give to her husband. But, Madame, continue and tell me who it is you wish to avoid at court."

"I beg you not to ask me that," she said. "Prudence forbids me to mention his name."

"Have no fear, Madame," said Monsieur de Clèves. "I am too experienced in the ways of the world to suppose that friendship with the husband would prevent someone from falling in love with his wife. One ought to hate this person, but not complain. Madame, once more, please tell me what I want to know."

"You would beg me in vain," she replied. "I do have the courage to be silent when I think I should. The confession I have just made to you was not out of weakness. It required more courage to rid my conscience of it than to bury it where you couldn't see it."

Monsieur de Nemours did not miss a word of this conversation, and what Madame de Clèves had just said scarcely made him less jealous than her husband. He was so madly in love with her that he believed everyone else was too. It was true he had several rivals, but he fancied there were even more of them. He searched his mind for the person she could mean. He had believed that he was attractive to her, but he had based his judgment many times on such trivialities that at this moment he could not imagine he had aroused such violent passion that it had recourse to a remedy as strange as this. He was so moved he hardly understood what he saw. He could not forgive Monsieur de Clèves for not pressing his wife more to mention her lover's name.

Monsieur de Clèves did make, however, every effort to find out. After he had tried in vain, she said, "It seems to me you ought to be satisfied with my sincerity. Please don't ask me anything more and don't give me reason to repent what I have just done. Be assured further that, by none of my actions, have my feelings been made known, and that no one has ever said anything to me which could offend me."

"Madame, I can't believe you! I remember how embarrassed you were the day your portrait was lost. You have given, Madame, you have given this portrait away—this portrait which was so precious to me and so rightfully mine. You could not hide your feelings. You are in love, and everyone knows it. It is only your virtue you have saved!"

"Stop," she cried out. "How can you possibly think that there is something artfully hidden in my confession? Did I have to confess at all? Believe me, I have paid a high price already for the confidence I have put in you. Believe me, I beg you. I did not give away my portrait. It is true I saw someone take it, but I pretended not to see him for fear he might approach me and say things that up to that time he had not dared to say."

"Then how has he made known he loves you? What signs of love has he given you?" asked Monsieur de Clèves.

"Spare me the anguish," she replied, "of going over all these little details which I am ashamed to have noticed, and which made me only too aware of my weakness."

"You are right, Madame," he said. "I am unfair. Refuse me always when I ask you for such information."

At this moment, some of the servants who had been along the paths, came to tell Monsieur de Clèves that a gentleman from the king had just come looking for him, requesting his presence that evening in Paris. Monsieur de Clèves was forced to go immediately, and he could say nothing more to his wife, except that she should come to Paris the following day. He implored her to believe that, although he was saddened, he still loved and esteemed her very much.

When her husband had gone and she was alone to reflect on what she had just done, she was so upset she could hardly believe it true. She thought that she had quite destroyed his heart and esteem, and had hollowed herself an abyss from which she would never escape. She asked herself why? Why had she done such a foolhardy thing? And she discovered that she had done it without really intending to. The singularity of such a confession—the like of which she had never heard—made her realize all the more its dangers.

But when she thought that this acknowledgment offered her the only means of protecting herself against Monsieur de Nemours, she was not sorry for the risk she had taken. She spent the night, full of incertitude, anxiety, and fear, but at last, in peace, in calm, and even in sweetness for having given to her husband who merited them proofs of her fidelity. The manner in which he received her confession showed his esteem and affection for her.

Meanwhile, Monsieur de Nemours left his hiding place where he had overheard their conversation, which so obviously concerned him, and plunged back into the forest. What Madame de Clèves had said about her portrait revived his spirits since it implied that it was he whom she loved. At first he abandoned himself to joy, but it was short-lived because in a moment he reflected that this same conversation, which had just revealed her love for him, also convinced him that he would never receive any outward indication of it. It was inconceivable for him to get involved with a woman whose scruples were so extreme. And yet he felt a keen pleasure in having reduced this woman to this extremity. He felt there was something glorious in having won the love of a woman so different from all others. Finally, he was a hundred times happy and unhappy at the same time.

Darkness fell while he was still in the forest. He had a lot of difficulty finding the road back to his sister's. He arrived toward dawn. It was rather difficult explaining what had detained him. He got out of it as best he could and hastened back to Paris with the vidame that very day.

This prince was so filled with his love and so overjoyed by all that he had overheard, that he fell into an indiscretion quite common, namely, to speak in general terms of personal experiences—to tell of one's own adventures using borrowed names. On the way back to Paris, Monsieur de Nemours turned the conversation to the subject of love, exaggerating the pleasure of being in love with a person worthy of such love and speaking of love's strange alchemy.

Later, unable to contain his amazement at what Madame de Clèves had done, he told the story to the vidame, without naming the persons or mentioning to him that he himself was a principal character. But Monsieur de Nemours told this story with such warm feeling and deep admiration that the vidame easily guessed the story was about De Nemours himself. The vidame chided him to own up to it, saying that he had known for a long time that his friend was in love and that it was unfair to distrust the vidame who had a while back entrusted him with the secret of his life. But Monsieur de Nemours was too much in love to confess it, so had kept it a secret from the vidame, although he was, in fact, his closest friend at court. Monsieur de Nemours replied that one of his friends had told him of this escapade and had made him swear never to divulge the secret; he begged the vidame never to tell this to anyone. Nevertheless, Monsieur de Nemours was rather sorry for having told him so much.

Meanwhile, Monsieur de Clèves had gone to find the king, his heart filled with bitter sorrow. Never had a husband so passionately loved his wife nor respected her so much. What he had just learned did not destroy his esteem but fostered in him a respect of a different kind. Now he must be concerned with guessing who it was who knew how to win a place in her heart. He first thought of Monsieur de Nemours, since he was the most eligible man at court. Then, he thought of the Chevalier de Guise and the Maréchal de Saint-André both of whom had wanted to please her, both of whom were still paying her much attention. He stopped giving any more thought to the matter, deciding it must be one of these three.

He arrived at the Louvre, and the king led him immediately to his chambers to tell him that he had been chosen to escort Madame Élisabeth to Spain, that there was no one who could better discharge this commission, that no one would bring more honor to the court of France than Madame de Clèves. Monsieur de Clèves received the honor of this choice as he should, viewing it as an opportunity to take his wife from court without there appearing too much of a change in her behavior. Nevertheless, the time of departure was still too far off to be any help in his immediate problem. He wrote promptly to Madame de Clèves informing her of the king's wishes and reiterating his pleas that she return to Paris.

She came as he ordered, but when they saw each other again, they were very sad. Like the true gentleman he was and worthy of the trust she had put in him, Monsieur de Clèves spoke: "I am not distressed over your conduct. You have more strength and more virtue than you realize. Also it is not fear of the future that rends my heart. I am sorry only to see another succeed where I have failed."

"I do not know what to answer," she said to him. "When I speak with you, I die a thousand shameful deaths. Spare me, I entreat you, these tormenting conversations; order my conduct, see to it that I visit with no one. This is all I ask of you. But be kind enough not to speak to me any more about this matter that makes me feel so ashamed of myself and so unworthy of your goodness."

"You are right, Madame," he replied. "I am taking advantage of your sweetness and your trust. But also, Madame, have some compassion for the state into which you have plunged me. Realize, Madame, although you have confessed to me somewhat, you are still hiding a name. This piques my curiosity and makes my life at court difficult to live. I will not ask you to tell me this name, but I cannot help but confess to you that I believe the person who deserves my envy is one of three—the Maréchal de Saint-André, the Duc de Nemours, or the Chevalier de Guise."

She blushed and said, "I shall answer you nothing. I shall not give you any reqson by my words which might lessen or fortify your suspicions. If you try to find out by spying on me, you will embarrass me in front of everyone. In the name of God," she continued, "please see to it, under the pretext that I am ill, that I see no one."

"No, Madame," he answered, "it would soon be figured out that your illness was pretended, and furthermore, I want to trust you alone. It is the road my heart and my reason counsel me to take. In your state of mind, giving you more freedom to act, I have you under closer surveillance than in any other way."

Monsieur de Clèves was not mistaken. The trust that he put in his wife strengthened her more against Monsieur de Nemours and made her take more drastic steps than any restraint of his could possibly accomplish. She went therefore to the Louvre and to the queen-dauphine's as customary, and so carefully avoided the company and glances of Monsieur de Nemours that she almost robbed him of the joy he had had in thinking that she loved him. Indeed all her actions persuaded him to the contrary. He began to wonder if what he had heard was not a dream, so unbelievable did it all seem. The only thing which reassured him was the extreme sadness of Madame de Clèves. Whatever her efforts, she could not conceal that. Her behavior, so austere to him, only endeared her the more.

One evening, when Monsieur and Madame de Clèves were at the queen's, someone remarked that a rumor was going around to the effect that the king would appoint another great noble of the court to go with the Madame to Spain. Monsieur de Clèves had his eyes fixed upon his wife when they added this appointee would probably be the Chevalier de Guise or the Maréchal de Saint-André. He noticed that she had not been moved by the mention of their names, nor by the prospect of one of them making the journey with her. He then concluded neither of these gentlemen was the one whose company she feared, and wishing to resolve his suspicions, he went to the queen's room where the king was. He stayed there for some time, and then returned to his wife and whispered to her that he had just been told that it was Monsieur de Nemours who would go with them to Spain.

The name of Monsieur de Nemours and the thought of being in his company every day during a long journey in the presence of her husband caused her consternation she could not conceal. Wishing to give some explanation for it, she said: "It is a choice disadvantageous to you because he will share in all the honors. It seems to me you should try to arrange for another to accompany us."

"It is not the fear of my having to share glory, Madame," replied Monsieur de Clèves, "that makes you apprehensive of Monsieur de Nemours' journeying with me. Your annoyance is rooted in other causes. Your annoyance teaches me what I wished to learn. Any other woman would have derived joy from this information. But have no fears. What I have just told you is not true; I made it up to confirm what I had already suspected."

With these words he left her, not wishing to cause his wife any further embarrassment.

Just then Monsieur de Nemours entered the room and noticed at once the state Madame de Clèves was in. He went up to her and said softly that out of respect he dared not ask what made her seem more distracted than usual. Monsieur de Nemours' voice brought her back to herself. She stared at him, not aware of what he had just said, full of her own thoughts, and fearful that her husband would see him with her. Distraught, she blurted out: "In heaven's name, let me be!"

"Alas, Madame," he replied, "I let you be only too much. Of what have you to complain? I dare not speak with you, I dare not even look at you; I tremble when I approach you. How am I to construe what you have just said? Why do you make me feel that my presence causes you grief?"

Madame de Clèves was annoyed at having given Monsieur de Nemours an opportunity to explain more clearly than he had ever done before. She left him abruptly without answering his questions and went to her room, more distressed than ever.

Her husband noticed her depression; he saw that she feared he would talk to her about what had just happened. He followed her into her room.

"Don't avoid me, Madame, or the issue," he said to her. "I will say nothing to upset you. I ask your forgiveness for surprising you as I obviously have done. I am punished enough for it by what I have learned. Monsieur de Nemours was of all the men the one I feared most. I can appreciate the danger you are in. For your own sake, and, if possible, for love of me, you must master yourself. I do not ask it as a husband, but as a man who depends upon you for all his happiness, as a man who loves you more tenderly and more passionately than the one your heart has singled out."

Monsieur de Clèves eyes filled with tears as he spoke, and he could hardly finish. His wife was touched, and with tears streaming down her cheeks, she kissed him tenderly, sorrowfully, so that his mood changed and a smile broke through. For some time they remained in a silent embrace. Finally, they separated, not having the strength to say any more.

The preparations for the marriage of Madame Élisabeth were complete. The Duke of Alba arrived to marry her and was received with all the ceremonial magnificence that could be imagined for such an occasion. The Prince de Condé, the Cardinals of Lorraine and of Guise, the dukes of Lorraine, Ferrara, Aumale, Bouillon, Guise, and Nemours, accompanied by many gentlemen and a great number of pages, clothed in their finest livery, were sent by the king to meet him. The king himself awaited the arrival of the Duke of Alba at the first gate of the Louvre, with two hundred gentlemen-in-waiting led by the constable. When the duke approached the king, he wished to embrace his knees, but the king prevented him and made him walk beside him to the queen's apartment and then to Madame's, to whom the Duke of Alba brought a magnificent gift on behalf of his master. He then was taken to Madame Marguerite, sister of the king, and paying his respects on behalf of the Duc de Savoie, assured her that gentleman would follow in a few days.

Extravagant festivities were held at the Louvre to display the beauties of the court to the Duke of Alba and to the Prince of Orange, who had accompanied him.

Madame de Clèves dared not absent herself, however much she wanted to, for fear of displeasing her husband who ordered absolutely that she be in attendance. But it was easier for her to obey because Monsieur de Nemours would not be present. He had gone ahead to meet the Duc de Savoie. After the prince arrived, De Nemours was obliged to stay with him almost all the time to assist him in all matters pertaining to the wedding ceremony. Hence, Madame de Clèves did not see him as often as she usually did. Consequently, she enjoyed some respite from her inner turmoil.

The Vidame de Chartres had not forgotten his conversation with Monsieur de Nemours. It stuck in his mind that the story which the prince had told to him was De Nemours' very own. Hence he watched him so carefully and perhaps he would have gotten to the truth of it, had not the arrival of the dukes of Alba and Savoy caused a change and commotion at court to prevent his unraveling the mystery. The vidame's desire to know the truth, or rather the natural inclination we have to tell all we know to the person we love, made him divulge to Madame de Martigues the extraordinary action of this unnamed lady who had confessed to her husband her passion for another. The vidame assured Madame de Martigues that Monsieur de Nemours was the one who had inspired this violent love, and begged her to help him keep watch over this prince. Madame de Martigues was delighted to hear these words of the vidame. She had always noticed Madame la Dauphine's curiosity in matters that concerned Monsieur de Nemours and this made her still more impatient to probe the facts of this escapade.

A few days before the marriage ceremony, the queen-dauphine gave a dinner for the king, her father-in-law, and the Duchesse de Valentinois. Madame de Clèves, who had been busy dressing, went to the Louvre later than usual. On the way she met a gentleman coming to tell her that Madame la Dauphine wanted to see her. As Madame de Clèves entered the room, the princess called to her from her bed that she had been waiting impatiently to see her.

"I think, Madame," Madame de Clèves answered, "I ought to be flattered by your impatience. But undoubtedly your impatience is caused by something other than just a wish to chat with me."

"You are correct," the queen-dauphine replied. "And you will thank me because I am sure you will be interested in the story I have to tell you."

Madame de Clèves knelt down by the bedside, and fortunately for her, there was no light on her face.

"You know," the queen-dauphine began, "how hard we have been trying to guess what has brought about such a change in Monsieur de Nemours. I believe I have it! It will positively amaze you. He is madly in love, and loved in return, by one of the most beautiful ladies of our court."

These words Madame de Clèves did not relate to herself since she was certain no one knew of her love for the prince. A sharp pain tore at her heart, but she managed to say: "I don't see anything surprising in this for a man as young and attractive as he is."

"Yes, but that is not what is surprising," replied Madame la Dauphine. "The woman whom he loves has never openly declared her love, for the fear she had of not being able to control herself. What is more she has confessed her secret love to her husband and asked him to take her away from court. And guess who told all this. None other than Monsieur de Nemours!"

If Madame de Clèves was at first pained by the thought of having nothing to do with this story, these last words of Madame la Dauphine plunged her into the blackest despair at the thought of being too much involved. She could say nothing. She remained with her head resting on the bed, as the queen went on speaking, too occupied with what she was saying to notice Madame de Clèves' confusion.

When Madame de Clèves had composed herself, she said weakly: "It doesn't seem possible, Madame. I should like to know who told you this story."

"Madame de Martigues," answered the dauphine. "She learned it from the Vidame de Chartres. He is in love with her, you know. He entrusted this story to her as a secret when he had learned from the Duc de Nemours himself. True—the duke didn't mention the lady's name, nor did he even state that it was he who was the lady's lover. But the vidame has no doubt about it."

As the queen-dauphine was finishing her story, someone came over to the bed. Madame de Cléves was turned, so that she could not see who it was; but she surmised immediately when Madame la Dauphine, in a jovial tone of surprise, cried out: "Here he is! I am going to ask him myself about this story."

Without turning around, Madame de Clèves realized it was Monsieur de Nemours. She hastily drew close to Madame la Dauphine and whispered that she must not

speak of this adventure the Duc de Nemours had told the
vidame. It might cause a quarrel between them. Madame
la Dauphine answered with a smile that she was too
cautious, and turned to Monsieur de Nemours. He was
attired for the evening celebration, and with a grace that
was so natural to him, he began to speak:

"I think, Madame, that I can assume, without too
much temerity, you were talking about me when I entered. You were going to ask me something, and Madame de Clèves was opposed. Is that not right?"

"That's true," replied Madame la Dauphine. "But I
shall not be as accommodating to her as I usually am. I
want to know from you, sir, if a certain story which
someone has told me is true, and if you are not the
person who is in love and is loved by a lady of the court
who deftly hides her love from you but has avowed it to
her husband?"

The anguish and embarrassment of Madame de Clèves
went beyond what words can describe. Had Death that
very instant come for her, she would have welcomed it.
Monsieur de Nemours was more embarrassed than she, if
that can be imagined. This leading question by Madame
la Dauphine, who he thought liked him, posed in the
presence of Madame de Clèves, her most intimate friend
in whom she confided, and who confided in her, set up in
him such a confusion of strange thoughts that it was
impossible for him to control the expression on his face
The awful situation in which he had put Madame de
Clèves, the thought of the just reasons for hating him
which he had certainly furnished her, shattered his composure and stilled the words in his mouth

"Look at him! Look at him!" the dauphine said to
Madame de Clèves. "Judge if this story is not his."

Monsieur de Nemours, recovering and seeing the importance of escaping from this dangerous trap, suddenly
regained enough poise to counter: "I must confess, Madame, that no one can be more surprised or distressed

than I over the vidame's breach of honor in telling you this story about a friend of mine, particularly as it was a secret. But I shall get my revenge," he said with a pleasant smile that almost removed the suspicions which the dauphine had just had. "He has told me secrets which are of no small importance to him. But I know not, Madame," he continued, "why you do me the honor of involving me in this story. I told the vidame the exact opposite. The characteristics of a man in love, I admit, but those of a man who is loved— Madame, really now, how could you?"

The prince was glad to mention something to the dauphine which could have some bearing on what had happened between them in the past. In this way he rerouted the trend of her thoughts. She seemed to know what he meant, or thought she did. But, without answering, she continued to make jest over his embarrassment.

"I have been disturbed, Madame," he went on, "by my friend's problem and by the just reproaches he could very well heap upon me for telling something which is dearer than life to him. However, he told me only half the secret; he didn't name the person whom he loves. I only know he is very much in love and is to be pitied."

"Why is he to be pitied if he is loved?" queried Madame la Dauphine.

"But do you think he is, Madame?" replied he. "Do you think a person who was really in love could reveal this fact to her husband? The lady assuredly does not know the meaning of love; she has made light of the attachment this person has for her. My friend could not be flattered by any high hopes that he is loved. But, wretched as he is, at least he is consoled to have made her fear she might be in love with him. I know he would not change his position with the happiest lover in the world."

"Your friend has a passion very easily satisfied," said Madame la Dauphine, "and I am beginning to think it is not yourself of whom you are speaking. I am almost ready to believe, as does Madame de Clèves, that this story is utterly incredible."

"I don't think really that the story is true," joined Madame de Clèves, who had not yet spoken, "and if it were, how could one be sure. It isn't likely that a woman, capable of such extraordinary behavior, would be rash enough to repeat it to anyone; and her husband wouldn't have said anything either, unless he be a husband unworthy of his wife's frankness."

Monsieur de Nemours, who saw that Madame de Clèves might be becoming suspicious of her husband, relished the opportunity to encourage her mistrust. He knew Monsieur de Clèves was his most serious rival, the lady's trust in whom he had to destroy.

"Jealousy," he pursued, "and curiosity, perhaps, to learn more than he has been told about a situation, could make a husband blunder into many indiscretions."

Madame de Clèves had reached the limit of her courage and strength, and, not being able any longer to bear the conversation, she was about to say that she was ill, when, fortunately, the Duchesse de Valentinois entered the room to tell Madame la Dauphine that the king was on his way. The queen-dauphine went into her room to dress.

Monsieur de Nemours approached Madame de Clèves, who wanted to follow the queen, and he said, "Madame, I would give my life to speak with you a moment. But of all the important things I have to say to you, nothing is more pressing than this: Please believe me. If I said anything which seemed to suggest the queen-dauphine played a role, I did it for reasons that do not concern her."

Madame de Clèves pretended not to have understood the prince; she took her leave without looking at him and began to follow after the king who had just come in. As a great many people crowded the room, she twisted her ankle in her dress and stumbled. She used this as an excuse to leave the place in which she did not have the strength to stay, and pretending not to be able to stand erect, she went home.

Monsieur de Clèves came to the Louvre and to his surprise did not find his wife there. Someone told him of her accident. He returned home instantly to see how she was. He found her in bed, but learned there was nothing seriously wrong. After some time by her bedside, he noticed that she seemed terribly depressed, and asked, "What's the matter, Madame? Is there something else bothering you other than the pain you are complaining of?"

"Yes! Never have I felt so low! How have you used the great trust I was so foolish as to place in you? Was I not worthy of our secret? And if I wasn't, was not your own interest a strong enough reason for keeping it? Was it necessary that curiosity to know a name I had no right to tell you should oblige you to confide this secret in someone just to discover it? Inquisitiveness drove you to this cruel imprudence; and the consequences could hardly be worse than they are. The whole episode is known; I have just been told about it, not knowing at first that I was the lady mentioned in the story."

"What are you saying, Madame?" he replied. "You accuse me of having divulged what went on between you and me, you are telling me this is all known? Well, I am not going to try to prove that I am innocent of having revealed this—you would not believe me if I did. Undoubtedly you have taken somebody else's experience for your own."

"Alas, Monsieur, there could not be another story like mine. No other woman would be capable of such a thing. No other person but me could have invented it. No. This is not a figment of my imagination. Madame la Dauphine has just told me the whole story; she got it from the Vidame de Chartres who got it from Monsieur de Nemours."

"Monsieur de Nemours!" cried Monsieur de Clèves with emphasis that indicated his exasperation and despair. "What! Monsieur de Nemours knows that you love him and that I know it?"

"You always fix upon Monsieur de Nemours rather than another," she answered him, "but I have told you, and I repeat, that I should never give answer to your suspicions. Whether Monsieur de Nemours knows the part I have in this story or whether you have assigned me to another role, I do not know. But anyway, he recounted my confession to you to the vidame, saying he had it from a friend of his who did not name the lady in question. This friend of Monsieur de Nemours must be yours too, and you confided in him to enlighten yourself."

"Is there a friend in the world to whom one would have entrusted such a secret?" replied Monsieur de Clèves. "To tell what one would wish to hide from oneself would be a large price for a bit of enlightenment! Think, Madame, to whom you have spoken recently. It is more plausible that the secret has leaked out through you than through me. You were not able to bear all alone the embarrassment in which you found yourself—you looked for comfort by complaining to someone who has betrayed you."

"Don't continue to overwhelm me with grief," she cried out, "and don't be so hardhearted as to accuse me of something which you yourself did. How can you suspect me? I confessed to you, but would I be capable or desirous of teling another?"

The confession made by Madame de Clèves to her husband was positive proof of her sincerity, and she denied with such vehemence having told the secret to any one else that Monsieur de Clèves didn't know what to think. On the other hand, he knew for sure he had not said anything; and yet a thing that could not possibly be guessed was known. Thus the secret must have been divulged by one of them. But what disturbed him most of all was that this secret was in the hands of someone and that it would surely soon be spread all around.

Madame de Clèves was thinking almost identical thoughts. She found it impossible to believe that her husband had betrayed her and equally impossible to believe that he had not. What Monsieur de Nemours had said about curiosity making a husband commit indiscretions seemed to fit the mental state of Monsieur de Clèves so exactly that she could only believe these words were not said by chance; and this likelihood forced her to conclude that her husband had abused the trust she had placed in him. Each was so absorbed in his own thoughts that for a long time they said nothing, later speaking only to reiterate what they had previously said. In mind and heart they drew further apart than they had ever been.

It is easy to imagine how they passed the night. Monsieur de Clèves had exhausted the wellsprings of his loyalty, seeing this woman whom he adored in love with another. His courage was spent—he had no more. He even felt that he owed no loyalty in a situation in which his honor and glory were so seriously jeopardized. He no longer knew what to think of his wife; he no longer knew what course of action he should advise her to take nor indeed what course to follow himself; he found all around him only snares and dangers. At last, after a long period of troubled indecision, he decided, in view of his forthcoming journey to Spain, not to do anything which would make people suspicious or even aware of his wretched state. He went to find Madame de Clèves and told her that it was not a question of determining which of them had not kept the secret, but of making everyone see that the story was a fable and had nothing to do with her; that he depended upon her to convince Monsieur de Nemours and the others of this; that she had only to act with severity and coldness toward this man who was proclaiming his love of her. He told her that only in this way could she remove this idea of his that she loved him and that it was not necessary to worry about what he might think, since, in the outcome, if she did not exhibit weakness, all his thoughts would be easily dissipated. Above all, he said to her, she should go to the Louvre and gatherings there as she was accustomed.

After so saying, Monsieur de Clèves left his wife without waiting for her answer.

She saw that there was a lot of good sense in what he told her, and she thought it would be easy to carry out his advice since she was very much angered with Monsieur de Nemours. But she did think it wouldn't be at all easy to attend the marriage ceremonies looking calm and untroubled. However, since it fell upon her to carry Madame la Dauphine's train, and since she had been chosen for this honor from among several other princesses, there was no way of absenting herself without causing a great deal of gossip and causing a lot of people to ask too many questions.

So she resolved to make a serious effort. She retired alone to her room to prepare herself and to give herself over to all these disturbing thoughts. What disconcerted her most of all was that now she had reason to be angry with Monsieur de Nemours and could find no way to justify it. She could not doubt that he had told this story to the Vidame de Chartres—he had confessed it; nor could she doubt, from the manner in which he had spoken, that he knew this story involved her. How could she pardon such an indiscretion? What had become of his sense of proportion which she had so greatly admired?

"He was discreet," she said to herself, "as long as he thought of himself as unhappy, but the success in this affair, however uncertain, killed his discretion. He couldn't bear to be loved without everyone knowing it. He told all he could know. I did not confess that it was he whom I loved; he guessed it and let it be seen that he had guessed. If he had been certain of my love, he would have acted in the same way. I was wrong to suppose that there was a man capable of hiding what flattered his ego. And to think it is for this man whom I thought so different from others that I find myself like other women—I, who was so different from them, have lost the love and esteem of my husband, who should have made me happy. I shall be looked upon by everybody as a person who has a mad and violent passion. Monsieur de Nemours knows it now. And to think it was to avoid these misfortunes that I risked all my repose and even life itself.''

These sorry reflections were followed by a torrent of tears; but however poignant her disappointment might have been, she felt she could have borne all had she been satisfied with Monsieur de Nemours' behavior.

As for this prince, his state was not much better. His blunder in having spoken to the vidame and its consequences agonized him. He could not recall Madame de Clèves' embarrassment and sore affliction without a sense of deep remorse. He was inconsolable for having said things about this incident which, although gallant in themselves, seemed to him, at this moment, rude and discourteous, notwithstanding that these things made Madame de Clèves understand he was not unaware of her affection. All he could wish for was a conversation with her, and even this he dreaded.

"What would I have to say to her?'' he cried. "Should I go to her protesting what she knows only too well? Should I make her see that I know she loves me—I who have never even dared to vow that I love her? Shall I begin to talk openly to her of my passion in order to appear to her as a man become emboldened by his hopes? Can I even think of approaching her? Should I dare embarrass her with my presence? How could I justify myself? I have no excuse to offer. I am unworthy of being seen by her, and I can entertain no hope she will ever see me again. By my stupidity I have given her more reasons to shun me than all those excuses she was looking for and perhaps would not have found. By my foolhardiness I have lost the happiness and honor of being loved by the sweetest and most estimable person in the world. But if I had lost this happiness without causing her such torment, there would be some consolation. Now I feel more the wrong I have done to her than the hurt I have done myself in her eyes."

Monsieur de Nemours was for a long time remorseful and conscious of these thoughts. The desire of speaking to Madame de Clèves kept coming into his mind. He pondered how he might arrange an interview. He thought of writing, but at last he decided that after having made this terrible blunder and considering the mood she was in, it was best to show a profound respect by silence, to let her see that he dared not approach her, and to hope that time, chance, and the feeling she had for him would win back her favor. He also decided not to reproach the vidame for his infidelity for fear the vidame's suspicions might be confirmed.

Madame's betrothal, which was set for the following day, and the wedding ceremony, set for the day after that, so busied the entire court that Madame de Clèves and Monsieur de Nemours easily concealed from the public their sadness and anxieties. Madame la Dauphine mentioned to Madame de Clèves only in passing their conversation with Monsieur de Nemours, and Monsieur de Clèves spoke to her only about what was going on at court, so that she was not as embarrassed as she had supposed she might be.

The betrothal took place at the Louvre, and after the festivities and the ball the whole royal household went to pass the night at the episcopal palace as was the custom.

In the morning the Duke of Alba, who usually dressed very simply, wore a garment of gold cloth, interwoven with the color of fire, yellow, and black, all covered with precious stones, and on his head he wore a closed crown. The Prince of Orange, magnificently attired, followed by his servants, and all the Spaniards followed by theirs, came for the Duke of Alba at the hôtel de Villeroi, where he was lodged, and then, walking in fours, they proceeded to the episcopal palace.

As soon as the Duke of Alba arrived, they went in procession to the church, with the king leading Madame, who wore a closed crown. Her train was carried by Mesdemoiselles de Montpensier and de Longueville. The queen followed, without a crown, and after her came the queen-dauphine, Madame the king's sister, Madame de Lorraine, and the Queen of Navarre, their trains being carried by the princesses. The attendants were magnificently dressed in the same colors as their queens and princesses, so that one could spot which their ladies were by the color of their gowns. They mounted the platform which had been especially built in the church, and then the marriage ceremony was performed.

Afterward, all returned to dine at the episcopal palace, and toward five o'clock they left to go to the palace where a reception for parliament, the royal households, and the dignitaries of state was given. The king, the queens, the princes, and princesses ate at the marble table in the great hall of the palace, the Duke of Alba seated next to the new Queen of Spain. Below the steps of the marble table, to the right of the king, was a table for the ambassadors, archbishops, and knights of the order, and on the other side a table for the members of parliament.

The Duc de Guise, attired in a suit of ruffled gold cloth, served as the King's grand master, the Prince de Condé as chief steward, and the Duc de Nemours as cupbearer. After the tables had been removed, the ball began. There were intermissions for ballet dances and wonderful stage productions. Finally, after midnight, the king and the entire court returned to the Louvre. However sad Madame de Clèves was, this was not noticeable in the eyes of those present, nor especially in the eyes of Monsieur de Nemours, who thought her beauty incomparable. He did not dare speak to her, although the occasion of this ceremony had afforded him many opportunities. But he did let her see how sad he was and how fearful he was to approach her, so clearly that she no longer thought him so blameworthy for what had happened, even though he had done nothing to justify himself. On succeeding days his conduct was the same, and it made the same impression on Madame de Clèves.

At last, the day of the tournament arrived. The queens betook themselves to the galleries and onto the platforms which had been designated for them. The four challengers appeared at the end of the list, with a great number of horses and servants, making the most splendid sight that had ever been seen in France.

The king had no other colors but white and black, which he always wore in deference to Madame de Valentinois, who was a widow. The Duke of Ferrara and his retinue wore yellow and red. Monsieur de Guise appeared in rose-pink and white. At first no one knew why he wore these colors, then it was remembered they were those of young beauty whom he had loved before she was married, and whom he loved still, though he no longer dared to let it be known to her. Monsieur de Nemours was in yellow and black; everyone sought in vain for the reason. But Madame de Clèves guessed without any difficulty; she remembered having remarked in front of him that she was partial to yellow and was sorry that being blonde she could not wear it. The prince thought therefore he could appear wearing this color without indiscretion. Madame de Clèves was not wearing yellow, and no one could suspect that it was her color.

Never had four challengers performed with such expertness. Although the king was considered the best equestrian in the kingdom, it was difficult to decide who really was best. Monsieur de Nemours had a certain grace in all his actions that persons less interested than Madame de Clèves might be inclined to lean in his favor. As soon as Madame de Clèves caught sight of him at the far end of the list she felt an extraordinary emotion, and in all the events he won she could hardly conceal her joy.

Toward evening, when all was nearly finished and everyone was ready to leave, the king, to the great misfortune of the realm, wished to break another lance. He ordered the Comte de Montgomery, who was extremely adroit, to enter the list. The count begged the king to dispense with him and put forth all the excuses he could think of, but the king, almost angered, made him give in. The queen begged the king not to run any more, that he had done so well he ought to be satisfied with his successes. She entreated him to come and be with her. He replied that it was for her love that he was going to enter the race once more. He went into the lists. She sent the Duc de Savoie to beg him a second time to come back, but in vain. He fought; the lances were broken; and a splinter from the Comte de Montgomery's lance flew into his eye and stayed there. The prince fell from the blow; his equerries and Monsieur de Montmorency, one of the field judges, ran to him. They were dumbfounded to see him so wounded; but the king was not excited at all. He said that it was nothing and that he forgave the Comte de Montgomery. You can judge what consternation and sorrow this terrible accident brought to a day destined for joy.

As soon as the king was carried to his bed, doctors came and diagnosed the wound to be very serious. Monsieur le Connétable now remembered the prophecy that had been made to the king, that he would be killed in single combat, and he did not doubt that the prediction was about to come true.

The King of Spain, who was then in Brussels, being informed of the accident, sent his own physician, a man of great reputation; but he held no hope for the king.

A court as divided and distended with so many opposing interests as this one was in no mean state of confusion on the eve of such a momentous event. Nevertheless, all the maneuverings were hidden, and everyone appeared nervously occupied only with the king's health. The queens, the princes, and the princesses almost never left his antechamber.

Madame de Clèves, knowing that she was obliged to be there, realized that she would meet Monsieur de Nemours. She knew that she couldn't hide from her husband the embarrassment these meetings caused her. She considered also that the very presence of this prince somehow cleared him in her eyes and destroyed all her former resolutions. So she pretended illness. The court was too preoccupied to give attention to her conduct or to ascertain whether she was sick or not. Her husband was the only person who knew the truth, and she didn't care if he did know. Thus she remained at home, little concerned with the great changes in the offing, leisurely occupied with her own thoughts.

Everybody else was with the king. Monsieur de Clèves came back at certain times to inform his wife of the latest developments. In public he treated her in the same manner as he always had; but when they were alone he was a little colder and more reserved. He had not spoken to her again about what had happened between them; she had neither the strength nor the desire to broach the subject.

Monsieur de Nemours, who had been awaiting an opportunity to talk with Madame de Clèves, was surprised and upset not even to have the pleasure of seeing her.

The illness of the king was so grave that on the seventh day doctors despaired of his life. He faced the inevitability of his death with extraordinary courage—all the more admirable because he was losing his life through a freak accident, dying in the flower of his youth, happy, worshiped by his people, adored by his mistress whom he loved madly. On the eve of his death, he married Madame his sister to Monsieur de Savoie, without ceremony. One can judge in what state was the Duchesse de

Valentinois. The queen would not allow her to see the king and sent to her for his seals and precious crown jewels which she kept. The duchess asked if the king was dead. When she was informed that he still lived, she answered, "Then I have no other master yet, and no one can oblige me to give up what the king has entrusted to me."

As soon as he died at the château des Tournelles, the dukes of Ferrara, Guise, and Nemours led the queen-mother, the new king, and the queen his wife to the Louvre. Monsieur de Nemours escorted the queen-mother. As they began to walk, she dropped back a few paces and said to the queen her daughter-in-law that it was she who ought now to pass first, but it was easy to see that there was more bitterness than good-will in this remark.

BOOK 4

❧

The Cardinal de Lorraine's influence over the queen-mother was now absolute; the Vidame de Chartres had fallen from her good graces. Nor did he mind this as much as he should have, owing to his love for Madame de Martigues and his new-found liberty. The cardinal, during the king's ten-day illness, had time to scheme and to prevail upon the queen to make decisions that would further his plans, so that, as soon as the king was dead, the queen ordered the constable to remain at Tournelles by the body of the dead king and to arrange for the usual ceremonies. This commission kept him from court and deprived him of liberty to act. He sent a messenger to the King of Navarre, requesting him to come as quickly as he could, so that together they might check the rise to power of the Messieurs de Guise which he saw as imminent.

Already the Duc de Guise was put in charge of the armies and the Cardinal de Lorraine of finance. The Duchesse de Valentinois was banished from court; the Cardinal de Tournon, a declared enemy of the constable, and the Chancelier Olivier, an avowed enemy of the Duchesse de Valentinois, had been recalled. In a word, the whole complexion of the court had changed. The Duc de Guise, in carrying the mantle of the king during his funeral ceremonies, held the same rank as the princes of blood; he and his brothers were unequivocally rulers, not only because of the cardinal's influence over the queen, but because this princess fancied that she could dismiss them if they annoyed her but that she could not easily dispose of the constable who was supported by the princes of blood.

When the mourning ceremonies were over, the constable went to the Louvre and was received by the new king very coldly. He wanted to speak with him alone; but the king summoned the Messieurs de Guise, and in front of them, told the constable that he advised him to take a rest, that high positions in finance and in the army had already been filled, and that when he needed his advice, he would send for him. He was received even more coldly by the queen-mother. She even reproached him for having said to the late king that his children did not look like him.

The King of Navarre arrived and he was greeted no better. The Prince de Condé, less tactful than his brother, vociferously complained—but to no avail. They banished him from the court under the pretext of sending him to Flanders to sign the ratification of the peace treaty. They showed the King of Navarre a forged letter which supposedly had come from the King of Spain, accusing him of having designs on his lands. They made him fear for his own lands; finally, it was suggested to him that he should return to Béarn. The queen provided him with the means of doing so, putting Madame Elisabeth in his charge, even prevailing upon him to leave ahead of this princess. Thus, no one remained at court to balance the power of the House of Guise.

Although it was annoying to Monsieur de Clèves not to accompany Madame Élisabeth, he could not really complain because of the high position of the one who replaced him. But he regretted this task less for the honors that he would have gained from it than for the opportunity it would have afforded his wife to take herself from court without it appearing she wanted to.

A few days after the king's death, the court decided to

go to Rheims for the coronation. As soon as this journey was mentioned, Madame de Clèves, who had remained at home, feigning illness, begged her husband to excuse her from following the court and to allow her to go to Coulommiers for a change in climate and for her health. He replied he did not wish to probe whether her health prevented her from making the trip, but anyway, he would permit her to go to Coulommiers. In view of what he had already resolved, his decision was easily made: whatever high estimation he had of his wife's virtue, he realized that it was unwise to expose her any longer to the sight of a man whom she loved.

Monsieur de Nemours soon found out that Madame de Clèves was not to accompany the court; he could not go without seeing her, so on the eve of his departure he went to her room as late as rules of propriety would permit in order to catch her alone. He was in luck. As he entered the courtyard, he found Madame de Nevers and Madame de Martigues, who were just leaving and who told him that they had left her alone. He went upstairs in a state of nervousness and excitement, which was nothing compared to Madame de Clèves' state when it was announced that Monsieur de Nemours was here to see her.

Fear that he would again speak of his love, apprehension that she might reply too favorably, the anxiety this visit might cause her husband, the pain of rendering an account of it to her husband or of hiding it from him—all these fears flashed in a moment before her mind and plunged her into such a state of confusion that she resolved to avoid the one thing in the world she wanted most. She sent one of her servants to Monsieur de Nemours, who was waiting in her antechamber, to tell him that she had just taken sick and that she was very sorry not to be able to honor the request of his visit. What sorrow for this prince not to see Madame de Clèves. What sorrow not to see her because she wished herself that he should not see her. He left the following day; he had nothing more to hope for from chance. He had not said anything to her since their conversation with Madame la Dauphine, and he had every reason to believe now that his error in speaking too freely with the vidame had dissipated all his hopes; he left dejected and embittered.

As soon as Madame de Clèves had recovered a little from the agitation which the thought of the prince's visit had caused her, all the reasons she had advanced for refusing to see him evaporated; she even felt she might have been wrong, and if she had dared or if there had still been time, she would have called him back.

Mesdames de Nevers and de Martigues, on leaving Madame de Clèves hurried to the queen-dauphine. Monsieur de Clèves was there. The princess asked whence they came. They told her that they had just left Madame de Clèves', where they had spent part of the afternoon with many others, and that they had left Madame de Clèves alone in company with Monsieur de Nemours. These words, which seemed so nonchalant to them, were not so to Monsieur de Clèves. Although he must have realized that Monsieur de Nemours could find many occasions to talk to his wife, the thought, nevertheless, that Monsieur de Nemours was with her, and alone, that he could speak to her of his love, suddenly dawned upon him as something novel and something so unbearable that the fires of jealousy blazed in his heart with more heat than they had ever before. It was impossible for him to stay at the queen's. He went home not even knowing why or if he intended to surprise Monsieur de Nemours. As soon as he was near home, he looked around to see if there was anything that might indicate the prince was still there; he felt relieved to see that he was not. It was some comfort to think he could not have stayed for a long time. He imagined that it was not Monsieur de Nemours, perhaps, of whom he ought to be jealous. Although he really did not doubt that Monsieur de Nemours was the man in question, he struggled not to believe it. But so many things had already convinced Monsieur de Clèves that he could not long indulge this state of wishful incertitude He went straight to his wife's room, and after speaking awhile to her on indifferent subjects, he could not refrain from asking what she had been doing and whom she had seen. She told him. But when he saw that she made absolutely no mention of Monsieur de Nemours, he asked her, trembling, if that was everybody she had seen, in order to give her another opportunity to name him. As she had not seen Monsieur de Nemours, she did not name him.

Monsieur de Clèves then spoke in a tone which revealed his concern: "And Monsieur de Nemours? Have you not seen him? Or have you forgotten?"

"I did not see him," she replied firmly. "I was feeling ill and sent one of the servants to make my excuses."

"You were feeling sick, therefore, only because of him," answered Monsieur de Clèves. "Since you saw everybody else, why did you make an exception with Monsieur de Nemours? Why is he not treated like the others? Why need you fear his presence? Why do you left him see that you fear seeing him? Why do you let him know the power of his love over you? Would you dare refuse to see him if you did not know only too well that he can distinguish between your harshness and your rudeness? But why must you be harsh with him? Coming from a person like you, Madame, everything but indifference is indeed a favor."

"I did not think," replied Madame de Clèves, "however suspicious you were of Monsieur de Nemours, that you could reproach me thus for not having seen him."

"I do indeed, Madame, reproach you, and my reproaches are well-founded. Why not see him if he has said nothing to you? But, Madame, the truth is that he has spoken to you; if his silence alone had been sole testimony of his passion, he would not have impressed you with his love. You were not entirely truthful with me; you hid from me the largest part of the truth; you were sorry for the little of it that you did confess; you didn't have the strength to tell all! Of all men I am the most miserable. You are my wife, I love you as if you were my mistress and I see you in love with another man, the most charming of the court. He sees you every day, he knows that you love him. Eh! And how could I believe for a minute," he cried, "that you would overcome this infatuation you have for him? I would have to be out of my mind."

"I don't know," Madame de Clèves answered sadly, "if you were wrong in looking with kindness upon my confession or if I was wrong for believing you would treat me fairly."

"Well, have no doubts, Madame! You were wrong. You expected of me things as impossible as I expected of you. How could you hope me to be reasonable? Had you forgotten that I was in love with you, that I was your husband? One of the two would be enough—but both together impossible. Eh! What else are they not? I have only violent and uncertain emotions of which I am no longer in control. I feel no longer worthy of you; you seem no longer worthy of me. I adore you, I hate you, I offend you, I ask for your forgiveness, I admire you, I am ashamed of my admiration. In a word, peace and reason have gone out of me. I do not know how I have lived since you spoke to me that fateful day at Coulommiers, since that day you learned from Madame la Dauphine that everyone knew your story. I shall not be able to unravel how it was known nor what has passed between you and Monsieur de Nemours on this subject. You will never explain it to me, and I am not going to ask you to explain. I only ask you to remember that you have made me the unhappiest man in the world."

With these words he left his wife and on the following day went away without seeing her. But he did write her a letter full of misery, honesty, and sweetness. She answered it so touchingly, so reassuringly, of her past conduct and of how she would behave in the future, that, since it was based upon the truth and indeed expressed her real sentiments, the letter impressed Monsieur de

Clèves and restored somewhat his peace of mind, especially since he knew that Monsieur de Nemours was with the king and not in the same place as his Madame de Clèves. Whenever this princess spoke to her husband, the love he had for her, the candidness of her confession, her friendship toward him, and what she owed to him, all the bad impressions were driven from his heart as was the image of Monsieur de Nemours. But this peace lasted only for a short while, and then the image returned, stronger and more real than before.

For a few days after Monsieur de Nemours' departure, Madame de Clèves hardly felt his absence, then it struck her with a cruel, uncompromising force. Ever since she began to fall in love with him, a day did not pass that she did not fear or hope to meet him, and now she was sorely grieved to think that chance could not bring them together

She went to Coulommiers taking with her two large paintings which she had had copied for her from the original painted for Madame de Valentinois' beautiful house at Anet. There were represented all the wonderful deeds of the king's reign, among others the siege of Metz, into which all those who had distinguished themselves there were painted. Monsieur de Nemours was counted in this number and, perhaps for this reason, Madame de Clèves had wanted these paintings.

Madame de Martigues, who had not been able to leave with the court, promised to spend a few days with her at Coulommiers. The favor both of them enjoyed with the queen caused between them no friction. They were friends but not so close that they confided in one another. Madame de Clèves was aware that Madame de Martigues loved the vidame, but Madame de Martigues did not know Madame de Clèves loved Monsieur de Nemours or that she was loved by him. The fact that Madame de Clèves was the vidame's niece made her more dear to Madame de Martigues. Madame de Clèves felt them to be kindred spirits inasmuch as she knew both she and Madame de Martigues had secret passions. Also, she liked Madame de Martigues because she was an intimate friend of Monsieur de Nemours.

Madame de Martigues came to Coulommiers as she had promised. She saw that Madame de Clèves was living a very solitary existence. Indeed, she noticed that this princess took special care to be completely alone and to pass her evenings in the garden unattended by the servants.

She would go into the pavilion where Monsieur de Nemours had overheard her conversation; she would enter the alcove which opened on the garden. Her ladies-in-waiting and her servants would remain in the other alcove or in the pavilion, only coming to her if she called them. Madame de Martigues had never seen Coulommiers; but she was overjoyed by all the beauties she saw and especially by the exquisite charm of the pavilion. Madame de Clèves and she passed every evening there. The freedom of being alone, at night, in this most beautiful spot, made it difficult to control the conversation between these young ladies so passionately in love. Although they exchanged no confidences, they found much delight in each other's company.

Madame de Martigues would have had much pain on leaving Coulommiers had she not been going to meet the vidame. She left for Chambord where the court was assembled.

The coronation ceremony had been performed at Rheims by the Cardinal de Lorraine, and the court was to pass the rest of the summer at the newly built château de Chambord. The queen showed much joy in seeing Madame de Martigues, and after showing her pleasure, she asked her about Madame de Clèves and what she was doing in the country. Monsieur de Nemours and Monsieur de Clèves were present with the queen. Madame de Martigues, who had thought Coulommiers perfectly wonderful, told of all its charm, and elaborated upon a description of the pavilion in the forest, relating how Madame de Clèves took much delight strolling about alone a great part of the night. Monsieur de Nemours, who knew the place rather well, could appreciate what Madame de Martigues was saying. He thought possibly he could see Madame de Clèves without being seen by her. He asked Madame de Martigues some questions to enlighten himself further. Monsieur de Clèves, who had not taken his eyes from him while Madame de Martigues was speaking, thought he could fathom now what was going through his mind. Monsieur de Nemours' questions confirmed these assumptions. He did not doubt that Monsieur de Nemours was planning to go to see his wife, and he was right. Monsieur de Nemours was so taken up with his scheme that he passed the night devising means by which it could be executed. On the following morning, he asked the king's permission to go to Paris, pretending some urgent business there.

But Monsieur de Clèves was not fooled as to the reason for his trip. He decided right then to find out about his wife's conduct and to remain no longer in this awful state of doubt. He wanted to leave when Monsieur de Nemours did and to arrive at Coulommiers a little before De Nemours in order that he might hide himself and perhaps discover if this journey was successful. But, fearing that his quick departure might appear unusual, and that Monsieur de Nemours, being informed of it, might change his plans, he decided to trust one of his servants upon whose loyalty and common sense he could depend. He told this man about his predicament and of his wife's virtue up till then. He ordered him to follow Monsieur de Nemours, to watch him closely, to see whether he would go to Coulommiers, and to see if De Nemours would enter the garden late at night.

This gentleman, who was certainly capable of such a delicate commission, did exactly as he was told. He followed Monsieur de Nemours to the village, half a league from Coulommiers where the prince stopped. Monsieur de Clèves' man surmised that he was going to wait here until nightfall. The servant did not think it necessary to stop there with him. Instead he went past the village into the forest, to a spot where he judged Monsieur de Nemours would be passing. He was right in all his moves. As soon as night fell, he heard footsteps, and although it was very dark, he recognized easily Monsieur de Nemours. He saw him make a tour of the garden as if to check if anyone were around and to select a spot where he might easily make his entrance. The fence was very high and there was another in the back to bar admittance, so that it was rather a problem to gain access to this pavilion. Finally, Monsieur de Nemours found a way through, and as soon as he was in the garden, he had no difficulty determining where Madame de Clèves was. There were a lot of lights burning in her favorite alcove; all the windows were open. Creeping along the fence, he went up to the window with what fear and emotion you might easily imagine. He stood behind one of the french windows to see what Madame de Clèves was doing. She was alone and looked so ravishingly beautiful he could hardly control the wave of emotion that the sight of her gave him. It was warm, and nothing covered her head or bosom but her long disheveled tresses. She was on her divan, with a table in front of her, on which there were several baskets full of ribbons. She was choosing among them, and Monsieur de Nemours noticed that they were the same colors he wore at the tournament. He perceived she was knotting them to a very unusual Indian walking stick which he had used once and which he had given to his sister. Madame de Clèves must have taken it from her, realizing that it belonged to him. When she had finished her task, done with a grace and a tenderness that radiated on her face the sentiments she felt in her heart, she took a candle and went over to a large table which stood in front of the picture of the siege of Metz and in which the portrait of Monsieur de Nemours figured. She sat down and gazed with rapt attention at his picture as if overwhelmed by the love this picture inspired.

At this moment it would have been impossible to describe Monsieur de Nemours' feelings. To see in the middle of night, in the most delightful spot in the world, a person whom he adored, to see her without her knowledge, to see her busy with little things that concerned him, and displaying the love which she was trying desperately to hide from him. No lover has ever enjoyed such transports of joy.

He was so beside himself that he just stood there immobile looking at her, unconscious of the precious few moments left to him. When he was a little more composed, he thought that he should wait until she came into the garden to speak to her. This, he reasoned, he could do with a degree of safety since her servants would not be close by. However, as she stayed in her alcove, he decided to go in. But he couldn't bring himself to carry out this resolution. He feared displeasing her. He feared the sweet tender expressions on her face would change to anger and hate.

He reflected for a moment that he had been foolish, not in coming to see Madame de Clèves without her knowledge, but in imagining that he could let her see him. All the hazards that he had not envisaged while in Chambord dawned upon him. It seemed to him now that he had been too extravagantly bold in coming in the middle of the night, to surprise a lady to whom he had not yet even broached the subject of his love. He thought that it was foolish of him even to pretend that she would listen and that, for just reasons, she would be angry with him for the dangerous position in which he could by this indiscretion place her. All his courage failed him, and many times he was ready to flee without seeing her. Then, powered by his desire to speak with her, and reassured by all that he had seen through the window, he did advance a few steps, but so nervously that the scarf he was wearing got entangled in the window and he made some noise. Madame de Clèves turned around, startled, and, whether she had this prince on her mind, or whether she was standing where there was enough light to enable her to identify him, she thought she recognized him.

Without hesitation and without turning to glance again in his direction, she ran out of her alcove inside to her women. She came to them so upset that she was forced, in order to hide her emotions, to say she was ill. She said it, too, in order to busy her servants and to give Monsieur de Nemours time to escape.

But later, the more she thought about it the more she was ready to believe her imagination was playing tricks upon her. She knew Monsieur de Nemours was at Chambord, that it wasn't likely that he would do anything so dangerous. She wanted very much several times to go back into her alcove again and to go into the garden to see if anyone was there. Perhaps she wished, as much as she feared, to find Monsieur de Nemours, but in the end reason and prudence triumphed, and she decided it was better to live with the doubt than to take the chance of discovering the truth. She was a long time deciding to leave a place perhaps so near the prince, and it was almost daybreak when she returned to the château.

Monsieur de Nemours had remained in the garden as long as the lights were still burning. He had not quite abandoned hope of seeing again Madame de Clèves, although he was convinced she had spotted him and had left only to avoid meeting him. But when he saw the doors were being closed, he reckoned there was nothing more to hope for. So he went back to get his horse, very close to the place where Monsieur de Clèves' gentleman was waiting. The gentleman followed him back to the same village which he had left earlier in the evening.

Monsieur de Nemours resolved to spend the day there in the village in order that he might return that night to Coulommiers to see if Madame de Clèves would be cruel enough again to flee him or cruel enough not to allow herself to be seen. Although it was a real joy to have found her so filled with the image of him, he was nonetheless very dejected, knowing that her first impulse was to run from him.

Passion had never been so violent nor so tender as it

was now in the heart of this prince. He retreated under
some willow trees that were along the banks of a small
stream that trickled behind the house where he was hiding. He wandered off as far as he could so as not to be
seen nor heard by anyone. Then, of a sudden, he sur-
rendered himself to transports of love, his heart so overwhelmed with emotion that a few tears ran down his
cheeks—not tears of sorrow, but sweet, delicious tears
of a man in love.

He began to think back on all her actions ever since he
had fallen in love with her, dwelling upon her correct and
modest behavior toward him, although she was in love.
"For, really, she does love me," he said to himself, "yes,
she does, there is no question about that. The most open
promises and the very best of favors could not persuade
me more of her love than those indications which I have
received from her. Yet I am treated as if I were hated; I
had hoped that time would mend; now I ought not to
wait upon time. I always see her raising her defenses
against me and herself. If I were not loved, I should only
be concerned with making her love me; but I do please
her, she does love me, though she conceals it from me.
For what therefore do I hope? What change of fortune
ought I to expect? Beautiful Princess," he cried, "show
me your heart! If I could hear you state your feelings for
me but once in my life, I could bear forever after the
rigors of your coldness. Look at me once with the same
eyes with which you gazed upon my portrait last night.
How can you look upon it with so much tenderness and
still flee from me? What do you fear? Why is my love so
repugnant to you? You love me and you hide it in vain;
you have given me too many unconscious proofs of it. I
know what happiness could be; let me enjoy some and
stop making my life miserable. How can I be loved by
Madame de Clèves and still feel miserable! How beautiful she was last night. How could I have repressed the
desire to throw myself at her feet? Had I done so I might
have stopped her from running away. My respect would

have reassured her. Perhaps she didn't recognize me.
Oh, I am too much concerned which I ought not to be.
The sight of a man at such a late hour frightened her."

All through the day these thoughts lingered in the
recesses of his mind. With impatience he waited for night,
and when at last it fell, he headed for Coulommiers.
Monsieur de Clèves' gentleman, who was disguised so as
not to be observed, followed him to the same spot as the
night before. He watched him enter by the garden. The
Prince was quick to perceive that Madame de Clèves was
taking no chances on being seen by him again: all the
doors were shut. He circled the pavilion to see if he could
discover any lights; but there were none.

Madame de Clèves, guessing that Monsieur de Nemours
would return, stayed in her room. She dreaded the thought
that she might not always have the courage to run from
him, and she did not wish to put herself haphazardly in a
situation that might otherwise compromise her till-now
correct behavior.

Although Monsieur de Nemours entertained no hope
whatever of seeing her, he could not leave the spot where
she so often came. He spent the whole night in the
garden and found some consolation, at least, feasting his
eyes on the same objects she viewed every day. The sun
rose before he thought of leaving, but at last fear of
being discovered obliged him to steal away.

It was simply impossible that he should go away without seeing her. He hastened to Madame de Mercoeur,
who was at home in her house near Coulommiers. The
unexpected arrival of her brother startled her. He fabri-
cated a reason for his trip that was plausible enough to
fool her, and very cleverly he schemed her into suggest-
ing a visit with Madame de Clèves. That very day the
suggestion was carried out. Monsieur de Nemours informed his sister that he would have to take leave of her
at Coulommiers to return as quickly as possible to the
king, thinking that by saying this, his sister might leave

first and afford him an opportunity to talk with Madame
de Clèves alone.

When they arrived, she was walking in the large path
which skirted the flower garden. The sight of Monsieur
de Nemours made her heart skip a beat, and she had no
doubt now that it was he whom she had seen two nights
ago. Because of the certainty of this conviction, the boldness and impudence of his actions somewhat angered
her. The Prince detected a look of coldness on her face
and was disappointed. They talked of general subjects,
but his conversation was so charmingly witty, so compli-
mentary, and so full of admiration for Madame de Clèves
that, in spite of herself, some of the coldness she displayed to him in the beginning began to lessen.

When he felt reassured, he expressed a curiosity to see
the pavilion in the forest. He raved about it as the most
delightful corner in the world and even described it in
terms so detailed that Madame de Mercoeur remarked
he must have been there many times to be so familiar
with all its beauties.

"But I hardly think so," replied Madame de Clèves.
"The place has just been recently finished. Monsieur de
Nemours could not have been there."

"Oh, it is not such a long time ago that I was there,"
contradicted Monsieur de Nemours, glancing at her.
"Should I be pleased that you have forgotten seeing me
there?"

Madame de Mercoeur, who was enjoying the beauties
of the garden, was not paying any attention to what her
brother was saying. Madame de Clèves blushed, lowered
her eyes, and said without looking at him:

"I don't remember at all having seen you. If you have
been there, then it was without my knowledge."

"It is true, Madame," replied Monsieur de Nemours,
"that I was there without your permission, but I spent
there in your garden the most wonderful, the most painful moments of my life."

Madame de Clèves understood only too well the import of his words, but she answered nothing. She was thinking how to prevent Madame de Mercoeur from entering the alcove because Monsieur de Nemours' portrait was there and she did not want her to see it. She succeeded. Time passed pleasantly until Madame de Mercoeur spoke of going home. But when Madame de Clèves saw that Monsieur de Nemours and his sister were not leaving together, she realized what was going to happen, and she found herself in the same embarrassing situation as she had been in once before in Paris. She made the same decision also that she made then. The fear that this visit would be only one more confirmation of her husband's suspicions helped her to act without hesitation. To avoid his company privately, she said to Madame de Mercoeur she would go with her to the edge of the forest and would order her carriage to follow her. The anguish which Monsieur de Nemours felt, seeing her pursue her strict line of conduct toward him, caused him to turn pale, so much so that Madame de Mercoeur asked if he was not feeling well. He glanced up at Madame de Clèves without anyone else in the area noticing and communicated by his soulful looks that despair was his only illness. For all that, she let them go on without following them, and after what he had said, he could not go back with his sister. So he returned to Paris.

Monsieur de Clèves' gentleman had observed Monsieur de Nemours closely all the while. He also went back to Paris and, as he saw Monsieur de Nemours leave for Chambord, he took the post so as to arrive there before him and give a report of his journey. His master was awaiting his return as though his life depended upon it.

As soon as Monsieur de Clèves saw him, he judged by the expression on his face and his silence that the news was bad. Monsieur de Clèves remained for some time. overcome with grief, his head lowered, unable to speak Finally he gestured with his hand for him to leave. saying: "Go! I see you have something to tell, but I have not the courage to listen."

"I have nothing to tell you," the gentleman replied, "from which any valid conclusion might be drawn. Monsieur de Nemours entered the forest garden on two consecutive nights, and on the day after he went to Coulommiers, with Madame de Mercoeur."

"Enough! That's enough!" Monsieur de Clèves made another sign for him to leave. "I do not need any further information."

The gentleman was forced to leave his master, who now abandoned himself to black despair. Few men with a soul as courageous and a heart as tender as Monsieur de Clèves', have experienced the pain caused by the shameful deceit of a wife, and this at the same time.

He was despondent, dejected, and totally prostrated, and that very night he ran a high fever with so many complications that right away he appeared dangerously ill. They notified Madame de Clèves, who came at once. He was much worse. Madame de Clèves noticed something cold and aloof in his manner which surprised and disturbed her. He even seemed to receive her attentions with glacial indifference, but then she thought this was perhaps the effect of his illness.

At first when she arrived at Blois, where the court now was, Monsieur de Nemours could not help being very happy knowing that she was near him. He tried to see her and called every day on Monsieur de Clèves on the pretext of learning how he was, but in vain. She never left her husband's room and was frightfully upset by his condition. Monsieur de Nemours was desperate seeing her so unhappy; he was fearful this affliction would renew her devotion for Monsieur de Clèves, and that this devotion would create a dangerous diversion to the other love she had in her heart.

This thought tormented him fiercely for some time; but the seriousness of Monsieur de Clèves' condition opened new vistas of hope. He saw that Madame de Clèves would perhaps be free to follow her own inclinations and that then he could find in his future a life of happiness and everlasting pleasure. He could not stand this thought, it troubled and delighted his imagination; he chased it from his mind for fear it would not come true.

Meanwhile, the doctors had abandoned hope for Monsieur de Clèves. On one of the last days of his illness, after spending a troublesome night, he said that he wanted to rest. Madame de Clèves remained alone in his room. Instead of resting he seemed uncomfortable. She went over to him and knelt by his bedside, her face all covered with tears. Monsieur de Clèves had decided not to tell her what he had against her. But the attention she was giving him, her sorrow, which seemed to him sometimes genuine and sometimes cleverly pretended, confused his mind and saddened his dying hours. He had to tell her what he was thinking:

"Madame, you are shedding tears over a death you yourself are causing. Your tears are shed for a pretended sorrow. I am no longer in any condition to reprimand you," he continued in a voice weakened by his sickness and regrets, "but I am dying of the mortal displeasure you have caused me. Could an action such as yours, which you confessed at Coulommiers, be without its consequences? Why inform me of your passion for Monsieur de Nemours if your virtue was not strong enough to resist him? I loved you to the point of being easily deceived, and I avow it to my shame. I have regretted this sham repose from which you aroused me. Why did you not leave me in this fool's paradise like that so many husbands enjoy? I would have been, all my life, unaware of your love for him. Soon I shall die," he went on, "but know this, Madame—you have removed death's sting. You have cut away the love and respect I had for you, and life would now be a horrible travesty. What would I do with my life? Live with a woman whom I have loved deeply and who has cruelly betrayed me? Or, live separated from her and do injustice and violence to my na-

ture and my love? My distress has been more violent
than you supposed, Madame; I hid it from you so as not
to inconvenience you or to lose your esteem because of
conduct unbecoming a husband. I deserved your love!
And once more I say to you I die without regret since I
could not have that love, nor do I wish for it any more.
Adieu, Madame. Some day you will mourn the man who
indeed loved you genuinely and properly. You will know
the difference between being loved, as I have loved you,
and being loved by men who, protesting their love, only
look for the honor of seducing you. My death," he went
on, "will set you free, and you shall have the opportunity
of making Monsieur de Nemours happy without committing sin. What does it matter what happens after my
death? It is weakness on my part to think about it."

Madame de Clèves, upon whom it had never dawned
that her husband suspected her of misconduct, listened to
all his words without understanding them. She thought
he was reproaching her for her infatuation with Monsieur
de Nemours. Then, suddenly it struck her.

"Me? Sin?" she cried. "The very thought of it is unknown to me! I could not have been more exacting with
my virtue, and I have never done anything that I would
not have done in your presence."

"Would you have wished, Madame," he replied looking at her contemptuously, "to have had me present on
those nights you spent with Monsieur de Nemours? Ah,
Madame, is it of you I am speaking when I talk of a wife
who passed some nights with a man?"

"No, Monsieur, no! You are not talking of me. I have
spent no nights, nor minutes even, with Monsieur de
Nemours. He has never seen me when I was alone. I
have never tolerated him or listened to him, and that I
swear to you—"

"Don't say any more," he interrupted. "These false
oaths and confessions equally pain me."

Madame de Clèves could not answer; her wounded
heart and her tears prevented words. Finally, mustering

all the effort she could, she said, "At least look at me; listen to me, you must. If it were only I who was concerned, I would suffer these reproaches; but your life is at stake. So listen to me, please, for your own sake. Is it possible, with so much truth on my side, that I can't convince you of my innocence?"

"Would to God that you could persuade me of it," he cried, "but what can you say? Was not Monsieur de Nemours at Coulommiers with his sister? And did he not spend the two previous evenings with you in the forest garden?"

"If this is my sin," she replied, "I can easily explain. I don't ask you to believe me; but believe your servants. Ask them if I went into the forest garden the evening before the afternoon Monsieur de Nemours came to Coulommiers; ask them if I did not leave the garden the night before that two hours earlier than I am accustomed to."

She then told him how she thought she saw someone in the garden and that she had believed this someone to be Monsieur de Nemours. Madame de Clèves spoke with so much conviction that Monsieur de Clèves was almost persuaded of her innocence. Truth is so easily self-evident even when the facts are not plausible.

"I don't know," he ventured, "if I should allow myself to believe you. I am so near death I don't want anything that could restore my will to live. You have explained too late, but what you have told me is a consolation and restores the esteem that I have had for you. I should like to have the consolation of believing, too, Madame, that had it depended upon you alone, you would have felt for me what you felt for another."

He wanted to continue, but he was too weak to speak. Madame de Clèves sent for the doctors; they found him almost without a pulsebeat. However, he held on a few more days, and then died with a remarkable peace of soul.

*   *   *

Madame de Clèves was in such an extreme emotional state that she was almost devoid of her faculties. The queen came to see her and took her to a convent without her knowing where she was being led. Later her sisters-in-law brought her back to Paris before she felt the full impact of her sorrow.

When she was strong enough to face up to it and to realize what a husband she had lost, and that the passion she had for another man was indeed the cause of her husband's death, it is impossible to imagine the horror with which she looked upon herself and Monsieur de Nemours. This prince dared not in the beginning pay any other respects to her than those demanded by convention. He knew Madame de Clèves well enough to realize too much effusion would be disagreeable to her; but what he learned afterward made him realize that he would have to be circumspect for a long time.

A horseman of his told him that Monsieur de Clèves' servant, a close friend, overwhelmed by grief caused by the loss of his master, had confided that Monsieur de Nemours' journey to Coulommiers was the cause of Monsieur de Clèves' death. Monsieur de Nemours was extremely amazed at this piece of news but, on reflection, he guessed part of the story. Then he clearly understood what would be Madame de Clèves first reaction and what an estrangement it would cause between them if she believed that her husband's illness had been caused by jealousy. He thought it would be best not even to have his name mentioned; he followed this course of action, painful though it was to him.

He made a trip to Paris and could not resist calling at her house to ask news of her. They told him she was receiving no visitors and that she even forbade them to tell her who called. Perhaps this explicit order was given with the Prince in mind so as not to hear his name mentioned. Monsieur de Nemours was too much in love to be capable of living so irrevocably deprived of the sight of Madame de Clèves. So he decided to find a way, however difficult it might be, to extricate himself from this unbearable situation.

The grief of the Princess went beyond the bounds of reason. The mental image of her dying husband, dying because of her, yet in the end so very tender with her, persisted. In her mind she went over and over again what she owed him and she thought herself evil for not having loved him passionately, as though it had been something she could have controlled. Her only consolation was thinking that she missed him as he deserved. She resolved that for the rest of her life she would behave as he would approve.

She wondered many times how he had known that Monsieur de Nemours was at Coulommiers; she felt reasonably certain Monsieur de Nemours had not told it to anyone. In any case, she did not care, so cured and uprooted was her passion for him. Yet it distressed her that he was the cause of her husband's death and she recalled how Monsieur de Clèves on his deathbed feared she would marry him. But all these troubles were jumbled in the sorrow felt for the loss of her husband. "Now," she thought, "nothing matters."

After many months she grieved less violently. She passed into a state of simple sadness and languor.

Madame de Martigues on a trip to Paris very graciously called upon her. She entertained Madame de Clèves with news of the court. Though Madame de Clèves seemed heedless, Madame de Martigues went on talking to distract her. She rambled on and on with news about the Vidame, about Monsieur de Guise, and all the other distinguished personages of court.

"As for Monsieur de Nemours," she said, "I don't know if he has substituted politics for love or not; but he is much less effervescent than usual and much less concerned with the ladies. He makes frequent trips to Paris, and I think, as a matter of fact, he is here now."

His name startled Madame de Clèves and she blushed.

She changed the conversation quickly, and Madame de Martigues did not notice her discomposure.

The following day Madame de Clèves, who was always looking for suitable diversions, went to see a merchant near by who specialized in making ornamental objects with silk. Madame de Clèves thought that she might do something similar. When some pieces had been shown to her, she saw a door to a room into which she had not yet been, and asked for it to be opened. The owner replied that he did not have its key and that the room was occupied by a man who came sometimes during the day to sketch the beautiful houses and gardens which could be seen from its windows.

"He is a man of the world and very handsome." he added. "He hardly looks like the type who would have to earn a living. Every time he comes in here, I always see him gazing at the houses and gardens. but I never see him working."

Madame de Clèves listened very attentively. As Madame de Martigues had said that Monsieur de Nemours was in Paris, she wondered if he might be the handsome man who came to her district. She had a picture of Monsieur de Nemours, scheming to see her, and this confused and troubled her in a manner she could not understand. She went to the windows to see what they overlooked. She found in view her garden and apartment.

When she returned to her room, she could easily see this very window from which, the merchant had told her, this man came to gaze. The thought that this man was Monsieur de Nemours radically changed her frame of mind. No longer was she in the indefinable state of sad repose that she was just beginning to enjoy. She felt again terribly upset and agitated.

At last, not being able to remain still, she went for a walk in a garden outside the suburbs, where she thought she could be alone. On arriving there, she found no one about, so she walked for a long time.

Crossing a little wood, she spied at the end of an alley walk, far from the garden, a kind of pavilion open on all sides. As she approached, she saw a man lying on a bench, to all appearances lost in his dreams. She recognized him to be Monsieur de Nemours. She stopped dead in her tracks. But the conversation of some people who had come along behind her brought Monsieur de Nemours out of his thoughts. Without looking to see who had disturbed him, he got up to avoid these people who were coming in his direction. Turning toward the other alley walk, and bowing very low, his courtesy prevented him from seeing whom he was leaving. Had he known who it was he thus avoided, how quickly he would have come back! But he continued up the path, and Madame de Clèves saw him exit through a back gate where his carriage was waiting.

What effect this view of a moment's duration produced in the heart of Madame de Clèves! The dying flames in her heart were suddenly fanned to life! She went and sat in the spot which he had just quitted, and remained there thunderstruck. Now she saw him as the most gentle person in the world, as a long-time lover whose passion was respectful and true, giving up everything for her, leaving the court of which he was the rage, respecting her grief to the point of seeing her without himself being seen, gazing upon the walls that enclosed her, and coming to dream in a place where he could not possibly hope to meet her—in a word, as a man worthy of undivided love, whom she loved so deeply that she would have loved him even if he did not love her. But more than this, she saw him as a man of the same social rank and station as she. Now there was no more duty and virtue to get in the way of her heart. All the obstacles had been removed; there was no more past; only the love Monsieur de Nemours had for her and her love for him counted.

All these ideas were new to her. The grief over Monsieur de Clèves' death had occupied her enough to pre-

vent her from considering these ideas. But the sight of
Monsieur de Nemours brought them back forcibly to her
mind. However, when she reflected and remembered
also that this same man, whom she now considered as a
marriage possibility, was the one whom she had loved
when her husband was alive, and the one who was the
cause of his death, and that even on his deathbed, her
husband had expressed a fear that she might marry him,
her conscience was so offended by these thoughts that
she concluded it would be almost as wrong to marry
Monsieur de Nemours now as it was to love him while
her husband was alive. She gave way to these thoughts
however contrary they would be to her happiness. She
fortified them more with other considerations about her
peace of mind and the prospective evils that might result
from marrying this prince. At last after passing two hours
in this spot, she went home, convinced that she must
avoid his presence as a duty to herself

But her conviction, a result of her reason and virtue,
did not drive him from her heart. She still went on loving
him so much that her state was really one to be pitied.
There was no more peace in her soul; she passed one of
the most restless nights ever.

In the morning her first impulse was to go to see if
there was anyone at the window which faced her apartment. She did so and saw Monsieur de Nemours. Surprised, she drew back so suddenly that the prince thought
she might have recognized him.

He had wanted her to see him ever since he first set
about scheming to see her. It was when he had given up
hope of realizing this pleasure that he went to dream in
the same garden where she had found him. Finally, unhappy and uncertain, he decided to try some means that
would reveal his fate.

"Why do I wish to wait any longer?" he said to himself. "I have known for a long time she loves me. Now
she is free; duty is no more an obstacle. Why tolerate

seeing her at distances without speaking with her? Has love so absolutely deprived me of reason and daring that I am any different than I was in other affairs in my life? I have dutifully respected her grief; but if I respect it too long, I am giving her time to forget what love she has for me."

Now he thought of ways he might use to see her. He thought that there was no longer anything to prevent him from revealing his love to the vidame. He decided to talk to him about it and to tell him of his wish to marry his niece.

The vidame was at this time in Paris; everyone had come to arrange his retinue and clothing in order to follow the king, whose duty it was to escort the Queen of Spain to her new country. Monsieur de Nemours therefore went to see the vidame and confessed quite frankly everything he had kept secret from him up to this moment, excepting that he did not make mention of Madame de Clèves' feelings for him, of which he did not want to seem to be aware.

The vidame was very much overjoyed with Monsieur de Nemours' revelations and assured him that, without knowledge of her exact sentiments, he had often supposed, since Madame de Clèves was a widow, that she was really the only person worthy of his hand in matrimony. Monsieur de Nemours asked if the vidame could arrange to speak with her and to ascertain her wishes.

The vidame proposed taking him to see her; but Monsieur de Nemours thought this would upset her because she still received no visitors. Both of them agreed that it would be best for the vidame to ask her to come to the vidame's house, on some pretext or other, and that Monsieur de Nemours should later arrive by a secret stairwell in order not to be seen by anyone.

It was done as planned. Madame de Clèves came. The vidame greeted her and led her into a large sitting room at the end of his apartments. Some time later, Monsieur de Nemours arrived, as if by chance. Madame de Clèves was surprised to see him; she flushed and tried to hide her embarrassment. The vidame chatted about many things, then got up and left the room, implying he had some orders to leave with his servants. He asked Madame de Clèves if she would do the honors and said he would return in a moment.

One cannot express what Monsieur de Nemours and Madame de Clèves felt finding themselves alone to talk together for the first time. They remained for some time in silence. Then Monsieur de Nemours spoke: "Will you excuse Monsieur de Chartres for giving me the opportunity to see you and to converse with you, which you have always so cruelly denied me?"

"I ought not to pardon him," she replied, "for forgetting my present situation and compromising my reputation."

She wanted to leave, but Monsieur de Nemours detained her and replied; "You mustn't fear anything, Madame; no one knows that I am here and a chance visitor is not to be feared. Listen to me. You must. If not out of kindness, then, at least, for your own sake to rescue you from the follies to which a love over which I am no longer the master would most certainly drive me."

For the first time Madame de Clèves yielded to Monsieur de Nemours, and looking at him, her eyes bright with tenderness and charm, said, "But what would you hope for if I obliged you? You would be sorry perhaps in the end, and I would repent having given my consent. You desire a happier fate than you have had till now and than you can have in the future unless you look elsewhere for it."

"I, Madame, look for happiness elsewhere?" he cried. "Is there any other happiness than being loved by you? Although I have never spoken to you, I cannot believe, Madame, that you are unaware of my love. I am sure that you know it is real, deep, and will abide forever. Do you know to what tests it has been put? Do you know to what tests your severity has subjected it?"

Madame de Clèves sat down and said, "Since you wish

me to speak and since I have decided to do so, I shall be honest with you and frank to an extent difficult with persons of my sex. I shall not tell you that I haven't noticed your inclination for me; perhaps you would not believe me if I did. Not only have I sensed it, but I sensed it in the ways you wanted me to feel this love."

Monsieur de Nemours interrupted, "If you recognized my love, Madame, is it possible that you were not touched by it? Did it not make any impression upon your heart?"

"You would have to judge that by my conduct," she replied. "But I should like to know what you have thought."

"I would have to be in a more fortunate situation to dare tell you," he replied. "All that I can tell you, Madame, is that I wish ardently that you had not confessed to your husband what you were hiding from me and that, on the contrary, you had hidden from him what you had let me see."

"But how were you able to discover," she replied with a blush, "that I had made this confession to Monsieur de Clèves?"

"I heard it from you yourself, Madame," he answered, "but in order to forgive my boldness in listening to you, recall if I ever abused the confidence I overheard. Think, were my hopes inordinately increased by it, and was I more forward when talking to you?"

He then began to detail how he had overheard her conversation with Monsieur de Clèves, but she interrupted before he could finish: "Don't tell me any more; I know now how you were so well informed. You seemed to be quite up to date that day at Madame la Dauphine's. She knew the entire story from those to whom you gave it as a secret."

Monsieur de Nemours then told how that had happened.

"Do not excuse yourself," she replied. "I forgave you a long time ago without asking for reasons. Since you have learned from myself what I had intended to keep secret from you all my life, I confess now that you inspired me with feelings which were unknown to me before we met and which I had no idea existed. Thus at first they took me by surprise and then increased the agitation which always follows in their wake. I make this confession to you shamelessly because now I am committing no offense and because you have seen my behavior has not been prescribed by my feelings."

"You must believe, Madame," Monsieur de Nemours said to her, at the same time throwing himself to his knees, "that I could die at your feet with joy."

She smiled and whispered, "I am telling you nothing that you have not known only too well."

"Ah, Madame, what a difference between learning it by some chance and learning it from your own lips! What joy to see that you want me to know of your love!"

"Yes, I want you to know of it," she said, "and I find sweet pleasure in telling you. I don't even know if I tell it more for my own pleasure or for the pleasure it gives you. For, in the end, this confession will have no consequences; I shall follow the strict demands imposed by duty."

"But, Madame, there are no more duties that bind you. You are free. If I dared, I would even venture to say that it becomes now your duty to cherish those sentiments you have for me."

"My duty," she replied, "forbids me ever to think of another, and of you least of all for reasons unknown to you."

"Perhaps, Madame, they are not entirely unknown to me," he answered, "but these are not valid reasons. I think I realize that Monsieur de Clèves thought me more fortunate than I actually was. He imagined without your confession that you had approved the follies which love drove me to commit."

"Please, let's not speak of this," she said. "The thought of it is unbearable to me. I am too ashamed and too saddened by the consequences my feelings for you produced. It is only too true you were the cause of his death; suspicions which your indiscreet behavior gave him cost him his life just as much as if you had killed him with your own hands. If you had met together in this embarrassing situation and you had killed him, what would be my duty? Yes, in the eyes of the world, it is not the same; but in my eyes there is no difference. I know you and I were the cause of his death."

"Ah, Madame," Monsieur de Nemours said impatiently, "what is this phantom of duty that blocks my happiness? What, Madame, is this vain, rootless thought which prevents you from making eternally happy a man you do not hate? I had conceived the hope of passing my life with you. Destiny has led me by the hand to the most wonderful person in the world; I have found in her all that could make for an adorable mistress; she does not hate me; I find in her behavior all that is desirable in a wife. For indeed, Madame, you are perhaps the only person in whom these two qualities have ever been found in the degree they are found in you. All who marry mistresses by whom they are loved tremble when they do so, and watch over them with fear, by reason of their past relationships. But in you, Madame, there is nothing to be feared; one finds only causes for admiration. Should I envisage, I say, such a state of bliss only to have you hurl in its way obstacles? Madame, you forget you singled me out from the rest of men. Or, have you never done so? Were you mistaken? Have I been flattering myself?"

"You did not flatter yourself," she replied. "Reasons for my duty would not seem so valid were it not that I *did* single you out among men. That is what makes me envision only unhappiness in loving you."

"I have nothing to reply," he said, "when you pose unhappiness as an obstacle. But I must confess, after all you have told me, I did not expect to encounter such a cruel reason."

"I want to give so little offense to you by my reason,"

replied Madame de Clèves, "that I find it very difficult making myself understood."

"Alas, Madame, what have you to fear after what you have just told me?"

"I want to speak more," she said, "with the same sincerity with which I have begun. I shall dispense with all the delicate reserve I ought to maintain in our first conversation together. But I beg you to listen to me without any interruptions. I think I owe your love the small reward of hiding none of my sentiments from you and of letting you see them for what they are. It will be the only time in my life that I shall expose my feelings to you. Nevertheless, I know not how to confess to you, without shame, that the certainty of not being loved any more by you, as I now am, seems to me such a horror that, had I not these insurmountable reasons of duty, I doubt if I could bring myself to face this unhappiness. You are free; I am free. The situation is such that the court would perhaps have no reasons to condemn us should we marry. But do men in marriage remain forever in love? Ought I to hope for a miracle in my case? Can I put myself in a situation where I watch this love upon which all my happiness depends come to an end? Monsieur de Clèves was perhaps the only man in the world who was able to remain constant in his love in marriage. Destiny did not wish that I should profit anything from this happiness; perhaps his passion lasted only because I did not return it. But I cannot use the same method to preserve yours. I believe obstacles preserved your love for me. You had enough of them certainly to drive you to win, and my involuntary actions, the things you learned by observation and chance, gave you enough hope not to be discouraged."

"Ah, Madame, I cannot remain silent any longer," said Monsieur de Nemours. "You are being too unfair with me and showing too much how ill-disposed you are toward me."

"I confess," she said, "that I can be swayed by my passions; but they do not blind me. Nothing can cloud my knowledge that you were born with all the qualities of a true lover and all the attributes that make for success in enterprises of this sort. You have already had many love affairs, and you will have many more; I would not keep you happy indefinitely. I should see you become interested in another as you had been in me, and I should be crushed. I have told you too much about my jealousies to conceal from you that you made me know what jealousy is. I suffered so much that evening when the queen gave me Madame de Thémines' letter, which was said to be addressed to you, that I know jealousy as the worst of evils.

"Either by vanity or by love all women long to win your heart; there are few who are not captivated by your charm. From my own observation I would say that there is no one whom you could not captivate. I would think of you always in love and loved by others, and I would not often be mistaken. In this unhappy state I should do nothing but suffer. I don't know even if I would dare to complain. We can reproach a lover, but can we reproach a husband when we have only to complain he loves no more? Perhaps I could accustom myself to this sort of an existence, but could I get used to seeing Monsieur de Clèves always accusing you of his death? Could I endure imagining him still reproaching me for having loved you, making me feel the difference between his love and yours? It is impossible for me to gloss over these compelling reasons. So I must remain a widow and hold firm in my resolutions to be such for the rest of my life."

"But can you, Madame?" cried Monsieur de Nemours. "Do you think all your resolutions are strong enough against a man who adores you and who is fortunate enough to please you? It is more difficult than you think, Madame, to resist what attracts us and those who love us. You have done so by an austere code of conduct which has almost no parallel. But this code can stand no longer in the way of your feelings. My only hope is that you will follow these sentiments in spite of yourself."

"I realize that there is nothing more difficult to do than what I have decided," replied Madame de Clèves, "and I mistrust my strength in spite of all the reasons I have advanced. What I owe to Monsieur de Clèves' memory would be a reason too weak if I were not more interested in my own peace of mind. And my peace of mind depends upon duty. Although I have little confidence in myself, I don't think I shall ever overcome my scruples; nor do I hope to overcome the feelings I have for you. It will make me unhappy, but I shall not see you again, whatever torture it may cost me. I conjure you, by all the power I have over you, not to seek opportunities to see me. I make evil what ordinarily would be permissible. Propriety forbids us to meet together."

Monsieur de Nemours threw himself at her feet and broke down completely. By his words and tears he bared the most sincere and tender passion which a heart has ever sustained. Madame de Clèves was by no means insensitive, and looking at him with tear-swollen eyes, she said, "Why must I accuse you of Monsieur de Clèves' death? Why have I just begun to know you? Or why didn't I meet you before he and I were engaged? Why does destiny keep us apart by an impediment so invincible?"

"Madame, there is no impediment!" replied Monsieur de Nemours. "You alone stand between me and my happiness; you alone impose a code which virtue and reason would never impose upon you."

"It is true I am sacrificing much to a duty which exists only in my imagination," she replied. "Wait to see what time will do. Monsieur de Clèves has only just died and this specter is too close to allow me to reason with clarity and precision. In the meanwhile, be consoled that you are loved by a person who would never have loved anyone had she not seen you. Believe me, the feelings I have for you will never change; whatever I decide they will live on. Adieu. I am ashamed of our conversation. But tell Monsieur le Vidame about it. I give my permission. In fact, I ask you to."

She left. Monsieur de Nemours could not stop her. Monsieur le Vidame was in the next room. He saw that she was upset and did not dare say anything. He went with her to her carriage without a word being uttered between them. He returned to Monsieur de Nemours who was full of joy, sadness, astonishment, and admiration. In a word, he found him full of all the sentiments which a passion full of fear and hope might engender.

It took Monsieur le Vidame a long time to find out what was the gist of the conversation between Monsieur de Nemours and Madame de Clèves. He managed finally. Though not moved by the same passion as Monsieur de Nemours, the vidame did admire, no less than his friend, Madame de Clèves' virtue, intelligence, and worth. They examined together the possibilities of the prince's fate; and whatever the fears his love naturally engendered, Monsieur de Nemours agreed with the vidame that it was impossible for Madame de Clèves to live with her resolutions. However, they agreed too that it was best to carry out her wishes for fear that, if the public noticed his love for her, she would make open declaration and follow a course of action, which she would be constrained to follow, fearing that the court would think she had been in love with him during her husband's lifetime.

Monsieur de Nemours decided to go with the king. It was a journey anyway from which he could not very well excuse himself, and he decided to go without making efforts to see Madame de Clèves again. He asked the vidame to speak to her. He wanted to say so much to her. He had since thought of a thousand arguments persuading her to overcome her scruples. Finally, it was very late before Monsieur de Nemours thought of letting the vidame go to bed.

Madame de Clèves was in no state either for a restful

night. It was a novel experience for her to have someone express his love for her and for her to express her love for him. She realized that she had acted outside of her self-imposed restraints. She did not recognize herself any more. She was amazed at what she had done; she regretted it; she was glad she had done it. All these emotions were fraught with trouble and passion. She reviewed again the reasons for following the voice of duty which was obstructing her happiness. She felt saddened that they were still so strong, and she repented having explained them so clearly to Monsieur de Nemours. Although the idea of marrying him had come to her as soon as she saw him in the garden, it was not so forceful as after this conversation. There were moments when it was hard to believe that marrying him would bring her unhappiness. She wanted to say that her idea was without support, that it was based upon past scruples and fears of the future. Reason and duty, at times, would point in opposite directions. But she was carried back to her original decision not ever to marry again; moreover, she resolved never again to see Monsieur de Nemours. But this was a hard decision to tell her heart, touched as it was and abandoned to these new charms of love. At last, for the sake of some repose, it occurred to her it might not really be necessary to take drastic measures so soon. Propriety gave her considerable time to make up her mind. But she remained firm with her decision not to have any meetings with Monsieur de Nemours.

The vidame came to see her and did as much for Monsieur de Nemours as he possibly could. He could not make her change her mind nor make her alter the conditions she imposed upon Monsieur de Nemours. She told the vidame she intended to remain a widow, that she knew this would not be easy, but that she hoped she would find the strength. The vidame was now convinced that she held Monsieur de Nemours responsible for her husband's death and that she considered it against her code of duty to marry him. The vidame feared it would be a difficult task indeed to unseat these convictions. He did not report to the prince her thoughts; he left him with all the reasonable hopes a man could have who is loved by his mistress.

They departed on the following day and went to join the king. Monsieur le Vidame wrote to Madame de Clèves, at Monsieur de Nemours' request, to speak to her about this prince. And in a second letter written to her a short time after the first, Monsieur de Nemours wrote a few lines himself. But Madame de Clèves, who did not wish to depart from her imposed rules of conduct and who feared the mishaps that could be caused by letters, informed the vidame that she would not accept any more of his letters if he continued to speak of Monsieur de Nemours. She told him in terms so clear that Monsieur de Nemours even asked him not to mention his name again.

The court went to accompany the Queen of Spain to Poitou. During this absence, Madame de Clèves stayed alone, and the further her thoughts were from Monsieur de Nemours and all that could remind her of him the more affectionately she thought of her late husband. The reasons she had for not marrying Monsieur de Nemours seemed to her strong now for duty's sake and absolutely insurmountable for the sake of her own peace of mind. The conviction that this prince's love for her would cease, and the evils of jealousy which she thought inevitably would arise in marriage, pointed out to her the certain unhappiness into which she was hurling herself. But she saw also that she was undertaking an impossible task in resisting the sight of this lovable man who loved her and in struggling against something which offended neither virtue nor decency. She reasoned absence alone and isolation from him could give her strength. She thought she had need of absence not only to sustain the resolution not to engage herself but even to prevent her from meeting with Monsieur de Nemours.

So she decided to take a rather extended voyage to pass the time propriety required her to remain in mourning. A large estate which she had near the Pyrénées seemed to her the best choice. She left a few days before the court returned. Before leaving, she wrote to the vidame begging him that no one should ask for her or write.

Monsieur de Nemours was saddened by the journey as another would have been by the death of his mistress. The thought of not seeing her for a long time grieved him very much. However, there was nothing he could do. but his sorrow increased day by day.

As for Madame de Clèves, who was so emotionally distraught, she became violently ill as soon as she arrived at her destination. News of her illness soon reached court. Monsieur de Nemours was inconsolable and desperate. It was all the vidame could do to prevent the court from learning of his secret passion and to keep him from going to find out personally how she was. Monsieur le Vidame. because he was an uncle and a close friend, used this as a pretext to send messengers. At last they heard that she was out of immediate danger but that she was wasting away and little hope was given for her life.

This thought of death, so close and so long lasting, made her see life with a different perspective. The necessity of dying—and she thought she was going to die soon—accustomed her to view everything with detachment. This detachment became a habit as her illness was prolonged. When she felt somewhat better, she found. nevertheless, that Monsieur de Nemours had not been erased from her heart; but she marshaled to her aid in a violent battle all those reasons she had for not ever marrying him. At last she overwhelmed her enemy—passion. Thoughts of death had brought to memory Monsieur de Clèves. This memory, which harmonized with her call to duty, touched her heart deeply. The passions and entanglements of this world now appeared to her as

they appear to people who have greater spiritual understanding. Her health, which remained quite delicate, helped
her stand fast in her convictions. But as she knew well
what happens to the best of resolutions, she did not want
to expose herself haphazardly to dangers nor did she
want to return to the place where the man she loved was.
She went, on the pretext of bettering her health, to a
convent, without any fixed intention of retiring from
court.

As soon as Monsieur de Nemours heard of this, he felt
the full weight of this retreat; he saw the seriousness of
it. In a flash, he knew he had nothing to hope for. But he
did everything he could to bring Madame de Clèves
back. He made the queen write to her; he made the
vidame write. He asked the vidame to go to see her. The
vidame did see her: she did not say that her resolution
was definitive. But he felt however that she would never
return to court. All efforts seemed in vain.

Finally Monsieur de Nemours went himself to see her
on the pretext of taking waters. She was deeply troubled
and surprised to learn of his arrival. She had him told,
through a person whom she liked and whom she had with
her, that she would ask him not to find it strange if she
would not expose herself to the dangers of seeing him
and to the danger of destroying by his presence feelings
she ought to preserve. She wanted him to know that,
since observing her duty and maintaining her peace of
mind were diametrically opposed to her inclination for
him, all the things of this world were indifferent to her
now and she had renounced them forever. She wanted
him to know that she was thinking now only of things
eternal and that the only sentiment left in her heart was
her desire to see him in the same state of mind as she.

Monsieur de Nemours thought he would die of grief in
the presence of this messenger who was speaking. Twenty
times he beseeched her to return to Madame de Clèves
and arrange for him to see her. But the lady said that not
only had Madame de Clèves forbidden her to bring back

any message, but also she had forbidden even a report of the substance of any conversation. Finally, the prince had to leave, as overburdened with grief as any man would be who had just lost all hope of ever seeing again the person whom he had loved so passionately, so violently, so naturally. Nevertheless, he was not totally discouraged; he did everything imaginable to make her change her mind.

At last, when years had passed, time and absence mitigated his sorrow and extinguished his passion.

Madame de Clèves lived in a manner that gave no indication she would ever return. She spent part of the year in this convent and the rest at home. She lived in retreat with more saintly occupations to busy her than those in the most austere religious orders. The short life left to her afforded inimitable examples of virtue.

SOME HISTORICAL NOTES
ON
THE PRINCESS OF CLÈVES
❦

Henri II and the Maison de Valois

Henri II (1519–1559), second son of François I and
Claude de France, is regarded as one of France's most
able kings, although, regrettably, his reign (1547–1559)
was brief. Acceding to the throne of France at the death
of his father, in 1547, Henri fell heir to the never-ending
French-German wars François I and Charles V had been
waging since 1519. By 1557 (when *The Princess of Clèves*
begins) the adversaries had tired of the constant warfare,
and one of Henri's last acts was to effect, in 1559, the
prudent treaty of Cateau-Cambrésis. Among its many
articles the treaty contained provisions—which Madame
de Lafayette, with a woman's heart, called *"les principaux
articles"*—for the marriages of Henri's daughter, Elisabeth de France and of Henri's sister, Marguerite de
France.

Henri's consort—the "queen" and later the "queen-
mother" in *The Princess of Clèves*—was the Florentine
commoner, Catherine de' Médicis (1519–1589), daughter
of Lorenzo de' Medici. Madame de Lafayette was kind
to describe her as *"belle"*; André Maurois said that Catherine was as "ugly as Diane [de Poitiers] was beautiful."
In any case, she was unquestionably an extraordinary
woman. Barren for the first ten years of her marriage,

163

Catherine redeemed herself by presenting France with an abundance of royal progeny: François de Valois (1544–1560). the sickly and delicate "dauphin," married Marie Stuart in 1558, became François II, King of France, in 1559, and died in 1560. Élisabeth de France (1545–1568)—"Madame the king's daughter"—became Queen of Spain at her marriage to Philip II in 1559 (she was the third of his four wives, succeeding Mary Tudor of England). Her sister Claude de France married Charles, Duc de Lorraine (1543–1608). The younger sons were: The Duc d'Orléans (1550–1574), who ruled France as Charles IX (1560–1574), the Duc d'Anjou (1551–1589), who ruled as Henri III (1574–1589); and the Duc d'Alençon. And the youngest daughter was Marguerite de Valois (1553–1615), famous as the beautiful and high-living Queen Margot, wife of Henri IV, King of France.

Among the charming ladies at Henri's court was Marguerite de France (1523–1574)—"Madame the king's sister." A spinster, she was rescued from her fate (when she was thirty-six years old) by the treaty of Cateau-Cambrésis. which provided her with a husband in the person of Philibert-Emmanuel, Duc de Savoie. And most famous of all the ladies—in the annals of art, at least—was Diane de Poitiers, Duchesse de Valentinois (1499–1566). An ex-mistress of Henri's father, Diane de Poitiers was the "inconsolable" widow of Louis de Brézé. Sénéchal de Normandie. The alliance between the youthful dauphin Henri and the beauty twenty years his senior remained unbroken until Henri's death, at which point the fair Diane was speedily dispatched from the court she had ruled by the long-suffering Catherine de Médicis.

The Maison de Bourbon

The *maison de Bourbon*, with the *maison de Guise* and the *maison de Montmorency*. were the three most powerful factions at the court of Henri II Antoine de Bourbon, Duc de Vendôme—Madame de Lafayette's "King of Navarre"—succeeded to the rule of Navarre in 1555 through his marriage to the strong-minded Jean d'Albret (1528–1572)—Madame de Lafayette's "Queen of Navarre" —who inherited the kingdom of Navarre from her parents, Marguerite d'Angoulême (François I's devoted sister) and Henri II d'Albret, King of Navarre. Louis de Bourbon, the powerful Prince de Condé (1530–1569), a brother of the "King of Navarre," was to become the leader of the Huguenots during the virulent religious wars that raged from 1562–1609, and would meet his death at an assassin's hands after the battle of Jarnac. In the religious wars the Bourbons espoused the cause of the Huguenots, while the Guises led those who sought to keep France a Catholic country. Peace was restored only when the then-flexible Bourbons achieved the throne of France: in 1589 Henri III de Navarre, husband of Queen Margot, the son of the "King of Navarre" and the "Queen of Navarre," became Henri IV of France.

The Maison de Guise

The *maison de Guise* was headed in the 1550's by two ambitious and determined brothers: the older, François de Lorraine, Duc de Guise (1519–1563), was one of the most illustrious military men of his time; he became a national hero when he defeated the forces of Charles V at the battle of Metz, and enhanced his reputation by the capture of Calais, the gain that finally and decisively ended England's foothold in France. His brother, Charles de Guise, Cardinal de Lorraine (1524–1574), perhaps the more formidable of the brothers, was a major figure in the religious wars. The younger brothers, the Chevalier de Guise and the Duc d'Aumale, play no such major roles in history. Their famous sister, Marie de Lorraine, or Mary of Guise (1515–1560), wife of James V of Scotland, ruled Scotland as queen regent from 1554–1559; their daughter was the ill-fated Marie Stuart

A major coup of the house of Guise was the marriage of Marie Stuart, or Mary Queen of Scots (1542–1587), to the short-lived François II. This brief interval as "Madame la dauphine," or "the queen-dauphine," was one of the happiest periods in the life of this queen who paid for her sins—or, perhaps, her errors in judgment—with her lovely golden head.

The Maison de Montmorency

The leader of the third faction at the court of Henri II was the connétable, Anne de Montmorency (1493–1567), one of the most famous connétables of France. At the time of Anne de Montmorency, the connétable was the chief administrator of the government, his powers including supervision of the treasury as well as command of the armies. The Connétable de Montmorency was killed at Saint-Denis in the religious wars.

The Court of François I

Madame de La Fayette's characters make frequent references to the brilliant court of François I (1494–1547), a true Renaissance king. François I, husband of Claude de France (1499–1524), succeeded to the throne of France in 1515, after the death of Louis XII, his cousin and father-in-law. In 1519 he was defeated in his effort to become emperor of the Holy Roman Empire, losing the title "King of the Romans" to Charles V, and more seriously, finding his kingdom encircled by Charles V's territories. For the next thirty years these gentlemen engaged in wars which involved much of Europe at one time or another.

François' mother, the ambitious and capable Louise de Savoie, was queen regent during François' imprisonment in Madrid after his capture by the armies of Charles

V at the disastrous battle of Pavia (1525). François' sister, the famous and learned Marguerite d'Angoulême (1492–1549), wrote the *Heptameron*, a collection of saucy medieval tales. The king's mistress was the influential Anne de Pisseleu, Duchesse d'Étampes (1508–1580). The unfortunate Charles, Duc de Bourbon (1490–1527), was connétable during part of François' reign. Deserting France in anger at property disputes instituted by Louise de Savoie, the Connétable de Bourbon went over to the service of Charles V, for whom he waged bitter military campaigns against the French; he met his death at the siege of Rome in 1527. The three sons of François were: the dauphin François, Henri II, and the Duc d'Orléans.

The Houses of Hapsburg and Tudor

Charles V (1500–1558)—the "emperor" in *The Princess of Clèves*—was probably the most powerful figure in Europe of his time. Grandson of Maximilian I, Holy Roman Emperor, and Ferdinand II of Aragon, son of Philip the Handsome and Juana la Loca, he held widespread possessions that posed a constant threat to France: he was monarch of Spain, the Low Countries, the archduchy of Austria, and the kingdom of Naples, as well as emperor of the Holy Roman Empire. At the time *The Princess of Clèves* starts, Charles V had already abdicated (1554–1557) and retired to a monastery. His son Philip II (1527–1598) inherited Spain, Naples and the Low Countries. The French-German wars were continued by Philip, who won the decisive battle of Saint-Quentin (1557), until they were ended by the treaty of Cateau-Cambrésis. The Infante of Spain, whom Madame Élisabeth once expected to marry, was Philip's son, Don Carlos (1545–1568). The Duke of Alba, the proxy bridegroom in *The Princess of Clèves*, is Ferdinand Alvarez of

Toledo (1508–1583), general of the armies of Charles V
and Philip II.

England, at the opening of *The Princess of Clèves,* is
ruled by the Catholic Mary Tudor (1516–1558), daughter
of Henry VIII and Catherine of Aragon. Bloody Mary,
as she was called because of the persecution of Protes-
tants carried out during her reign, was the wife of Philip
II of Spain. At her death in 1558, she was succeeded by
her half-sister, the Protestant Elizabeth (1533-1603), daughter of Henry VIII and Anne Boleyn.

Bibliography

❦

TEXTS

Lafayette, Marie-Madeleine Pioche de la Vergne, Comtesse de. *Romans et Nouvelles*. Ed. Emile Magne. Paris: Garnier, 1961.

ARTICLES

DeJean, Joan. "Lafayette's Ellipses: The Privileges of Anonymity." *PMLA* 99, 5 (October 1984): 884–902.

Danahy, Michael. "Social, Sexual, and Human Spaces in *La Princesse de Clèves*." *French Forum* 6, 3 (September 1981): 212–24.

Genette, Gérard. "Vraisemblance et Motivation." *Figures II: Essais*. Paris: Seuil, 1969, 71–99.

Haase-Dubosc. "La filiation maternelle et la femme-sujet au 17ème siècle: lecture plurielle de *La Princesse de Clèves*." *Romantic Review* 78, 4 (November 1987): 432–460.

Hirsch, Marianne. "A Mother's Discourse: Incorporation and Repetition in *La Princesse de Clèves*." *Yale French Studies* 62 (1987): 67–87.

Kamuf, Peggy. "A Mother's Will: *The Princess de Clèves.*" *Fictions of Femine Desire.* Lincoln: University of Nebraska Press, 1982.

Laugaa, Maurice. *Lectures de Madame de Lafayette.* Paris: Armand Colin, 1971.

Miller, Nancy K. "Emphasis Added: Plots and Plausibilities in Women's Fiction." *Subject to Change: Reading Feminist Writing.* New York: Columbia University Press, 1988.

Schor, Naomi. "Portrait of a Gentleman". *Representations* (Fall 1987), 20: 113-33.

Stanton, Domna. "The Ideal of Repos in Seventeenth-Century French Literature." *L'Esprit Créateur* 25, 1-2 (Spring-Summer 1975): 79-104.